RHODE ISLAND RENDEZVOUS

The Patricia MacPherson
Nautical Adventure Series
Book 3

*To the memory of Mary Ann Talbot
a.k.a. John Taylor
1778 –1808*

**Patricia MacPherson
Nautical Adventure Series**

Barbados Bound

Surgeon's Mate

Rhode Island Rendezvous

*"These resolutions, carried into execution,
the colonies cannot help but consider as a manifest
violation of their just and long-enjoyed rights..."*

Stephen Hopkins
Providence, 1764

*"There are limits, beyond which
if Parliaments go, their Acts bind not."*

James Otis, Jr.
Boston, 1765

RHODE ISLAND RENDEZVOUS

The Patricia MacPherson Nautical Adventure Series, Book 3

Linda Collison

FIRESHIP
PRESS

Prologue

October 1765
Aboard His Majesty's frigate Richmond
At sea, off the coast of the colony of Virginia

Brian Dalton nursed a fat head. Belowdecks in the gunroom, sipping his second cup of coffee, the frigate *Richmond*'s gunner stared vacantly at the jumble of initials carved into the tabletop, summoning the will to start his day. Four bells sounded. It was halfway through the morning watch; above, the decks had already been scrubbed clean and the men were setting the courses. He felt the slight lurch and easing over as the vessel adjusted to the increased sail and the resulting speed, his own spirit lifting ever so slightly like a pennant in the breeze. Those weeks ashore in colonial Norfolk were a drunken blur. It was good to be at sea again.

Gruen the bosun, his missus, and Smitty the carpenter sat around the table with him, spooning their burgoo sweetened with Barbadian sugar. The two men reminisced about their previous warrants, a much-worn topic. The bosun's wife said not a word but seemed lost in thought, not hearing the banter between her man and the carpenter, an ongoing argument about which ship had been the better. The young woman shifted the infant to her other breast, adjusting her cape for modesty, and smiled shyly at Dalton over the rim of her cup. He looked away.

"I've not seen Lily yet this morning," she said. "Is she well, Mr. Dalton?"

"I wouldn't know, Mrs. Gruen, ye must ask her yourself." *Damned women make much of nothing, always prying, always assuming.*

"There's been so many aboard come down with the sickness lately," she prattled on. "We never should have put into port; the air is much better at sea. You're a lucky man to have someone to look out for you like I look out for Mr. Gruen. He's never been sick a day since we've been together—have you, Mr. Gruen?"

The bosun didn't hear—or pretended not to hear—carrying on his conversation with the carpenter.

Bored with it all, the gunner drained the bitter grounds from the bottom of his mug, storing them in his cheek for something to chew on later. Then, summoning his will, he pushed his chair back and stood up, head pounding.

"My day begins. Good day to ye." Dalton's voice, like his head, suffered from last night's debauch. His throat felt like a dusty road.

He left the gunroom, bending his head under the low deck, and slipped his woolen jacket on, feeling the letter crackle against his chest. Her letter, written more than two years ago—nearly three— had just caught up with him in Norfolk, where the frigate had been laid up for repairs. She had written it a month after they parted in New York, explaining why she had not met him as promised, and he carried it inside the lining of his jacket for safekeeping. So much could have happened in all that time, yet the words penned by her own hand had fairly jumped off the page, burning themselves into his brain, and the memory of her voice rang again in his head. Ah, but it was nothing but a ghost from the past come to haunt him. He should drop the letter overboard. He would. No good could come of it now. Buttoning his jacket, the gunner went up the ladder for a breath of air.

"Good morning, Mr. Dalton." Goodwillie, the gunner's mate, ever cheerful. The best of the lot, in spite of his club foot and his diminished hearing. The two men had seen a lot of action together aboard this ship. "The breechings on number four are showing wear. Shall I replace them, sir?"

Dalton shook his head and barked, "Nae, we're low on cordage. Wasn't enough to be had in Norfolk. Serve them as best ye can with what we've got."

"Aye, sir."

Beer and rum, there had been aplenty in the taverns of the tidewater colony. And tobacco—there had been an abundance of that, not to mention a young woman the color of molasses with fleshy lips and a remarkably agile tongue. Couldn't remember her name, didn't want to. The frigate had anchored for a fortnight in the Norfolk roadstead, taking on wood and water and pressing a few men, and was now heading up the Chesapeake to Chestertown to deliver a lieutenant to his newly built revenue cutter. After that, the rumor (though no one but the captain knew for sure) was that they were to sail back down the great bay and out into the Atlantic, continuing north to patrol the mouth of Narragansett Bay— notorious for smugglers who operated by light of day, as brazen as you please. A preventive man's work, hardly worthy of a ship's crew that had helped win Havana.

The war, he missed it, the greater sense of purpose, with every man assigned a duty and expected to show courage in the face of death. The war was won and he had done his part to help Britain vanquish her enemies, emerging from his service alive, with all his limbs intact and a nest egg too—his share of prize money from the sale of enemy ships he had risked his life to capture. But the seven-year, far-flung conflict with France and Spain was history. Now his life was just patrolling colonial waters, harrying merchant ships, hoping for a payoff. There was little honor in it, and less reward.

At least my ship still sails. At least I have employment. A floating home.

The morning wore on. Another day to be endured.

A drumroll broke the routine, signaling the men to quarters. Dalton set off at once to his station in the magazine, deep in the belly of the ship. A rustling and thunder of footsteps as every man and boy hurried to his position, the gun crews assembling—a well-rehearsed maneuver that transformed the frigate from a floating city to a fighting machine. No matter that it was probably just a drill or a colonial fishing smack to harass, the rolling of the drum never failed to produce the same sharp sense of coming to life as it had during the war. A tingle of fear and thrill, a narrowing of focus, a heartbeat to keep pace with the drumbeat. Nothing like a good chase, the thunder of guns, and the sulfurous smell of burned black powder to set him aright. Duty and purpose, that was the cure. Norfolk, astern, just over the horizon. He had grown soft on liberty. Soft and restless. Had drunk too much rum and lost too much money on the dice. Dalton breathed deeply, blowing off the fog-like remorse in his head. Norfolk, where her letter had finally caught up to him.

Word came down they were chasing a Yankee merchantman suspected of evading import duties. It was easier to catch these buggers offshore where the frigate had the advantage of speed and firepower. Once they slipped into some shallow, backwater cove, the Yanks, with their local knowledge and their smaller vessels with greater maneuverability, had the upper hand. Still, he welcomed the hustle, the activity. Anything to break the monotony. It wasn't as purposeful as exchanging broadsides with a French warship, but a chase and a warning shot would be enough to clear his head. It would feel like old days. And he had asked permission to be part of the next gunboat launch, should one be necessary. That was something to look forward to.

The world was changing and Brian Dalton felt the years piling on, though he was not yet thirty. The war that had lasted seven long years had been over for more than two years. At first he had been relieved. Grateful to be alive, with all his limbs. His eyesight. Like his mate, his hearing was going—he was nearly deaf in his right ear—but compared to so many men he had come out well and was glad to collect his pay and his share of prize money. When the ship paid off he had taken a coaster for Whitby to see his mother and to pay his respects to his father, buried in the parish churchyard these many years.

He might have changed his life then. Might have left the navy and enlisted on a merchantman again. A collier or a fishing boat, which paid reliably, if not particularly well. So why had he returned? There was nothing in Whitby for him. *Richmond* was being sent out again to the northern colonies to deliver the new stamped paper decreed by Parliament for use—and to apprehend Yankee merchantmen suspected of violating the American Revenue Act along the way. This would likely be the frigate's last cruise, for she was getting on in years and was in need of a refit that wasn't likely to happen. The frigate was his home, his livelihood, his fortress, his mistress. Nae, his wife. He was her gunner; he would serve her to the end of her days.

Dalton entered the powder magazine—below the water level and pitch dark except for the glow from the light room where the lantern's candle shone. The magazine was his battle station: His duty during an engagement was to dole out flannel bags of powder to the runners who supplied the gun crews. As gunner, he was in charge of it all. He was a warrant officer, and the ship's thirty two guns were his pride as surely as if they were his own children. Still, he missed the action. Up on the gun deck, now that's where the thrill was—the ramming, the running out, the command of "Fire!" barely heard over the din, the deafening thunder, the terror and glory of battle.

The best part of his life was already over. He had a little money saved, not much. He had Lily, who mended his clothes, shared his biscuit, and gave him what a man needs. It was his privilege as a warrant officer to keep a wife aboard. Not that Lily was a church-wed wife; she was simply a wife by habit. Dalton wasn't even sure how and when Lily had slipped into his bed.

Now the other one was on his mind. The long-legged lass with freckled skin, with fiery hair and a spirit to match. He had discovered her in the bosun's locker, intent on Barbados where she hoped to inherit her father's estate. Of course, there was nothing for her there. Ah, but he had lost his heart to her, not once but twice. And then she disappeared—ran off—the night the frigate left New York. He had been hurt more than he cared to admit. When he thought of her, which wasn't often anymore, it was usually in bed, in the darkness with another woman whose warm thighs and soft moans he imagined were hers.

And now the letter had caught up with him. The letter explaining her disappearance the night the ship sailed. The letter professing her love. The old hurt felt fresh, a searing pain, and he wanted to roar, for it was too late to make amends. Now he had Lily, she was carrying his child, and truth be told that gave him a sense of purpose almost as great as serving his ship. The frigate *Richmond* was his mother, his country, his life, but the child was his future.

Once they delivered the stamped papers they would likely sail back to England and *Richmond* would become a hulk and he would become a father, a husband, a tradesman. Or, more likely, he would sail aboard a merchantman again, the only life he knew.

Providence Gazette; October 13, 1765

Last evening, well after dark, a straw man was erected and subsequently set ablaze on the front doorstep of the house newly occupied by John Robinson, appointed by the Crown to distribute the anticipated stamped paper. The tax is to go into effect on the first day of November, after which the official paper will be required for all newspapers and broad sheets, civil judgements and documents, shipping bonds and dockets, and every other recorded transaction. It is believed the effigy was burned to protest this heavy burden imposed on the Colonies against our consent by a Parliament who does not directly represent our interests. By the time the constable arrived the fire had burned itself out, leaving behind only a smoldering heap of ash. The perpetrators had dissipated, vanishing into the night. This latest incident is similar to a protest in Newport, in August. There an effigy of Mr. Johnston, the Distributor of Stamps, was tarred and dragged through the streets before being hanged from makeshift gallows constructed on the Courthouse lawn. The first shipment of stamped papers is expected to arrive soon from London—but after last night's mischief will Providence still have a King's man in residence to distribute them?

One

October 19, 1765
Newport, Rhode Island

It was a fine day for a wedding. Promising blue horizon, nary a cloud, the sun already trying mightily to burn the frost off the pane. I opened the window, called down to the water boy and hauled up a bucket after tossing him a coin. Then I pulled the shutters tight, lifted the shift over my head, and bathed quickly in the icy water, goose bumps rising on my skin.

I dressed in my best suit of clothing, clean and pressed. Placing the freshly groomed peruke on my stubbled head, I looked in the mirror hanging above the dresser of my rented room, adjusting the wig slightly. Acceptable. Yes, except for the ears—rather too small and pink—I passed muster. The only feminine feature about me was my delicate ears—and perhaps my pillowed lips, though they were often sunburned and wind-chapped. I regarded the young man staring back at me from the looking glass. Patrick MacPherson, a rising young merchant seaman dressed to go to a wedding feast where he will rub shoulders with Newport's best. *Good day to you, sir!* In this colony, anybody could be a gentleman if he had the means to dress the part. Here, the lowest-born man could rise above his station through cunning, hard work, and the right connections. Oh—and luck, I should add. Luck always plays a role. Thus far my luck had been most unpredictable.

The wig had been made from my very own hair, shorn from my head and at last tamed into submission by the peruke-maker's hand. Two smooth ginger-colored rolls just above my ears and a compliant queue held at the nape by a blue satin ribbon. A shaved head was so much easier, especially at sea, when all I needed was a snug Monmouth cap to keep the wind out of my ears. A shaved head was free of tangles, free of lice. My hair, perfectly groomed, kept in a box, ready for going ashore. No need for powder; no one in Newport bothered with powder anymore. Men were flaunting natural colors—black, brown, and auburn too—though none were as vibrantly colored as mine, the flaming red-gold of a Guy Fawkes bonfire.

I should have been born male, I thought with chagrin, regarding my reflection. I cut a fine figure in my pressed linen shirt, lace stock, and brocade waistcoat that completely hid my breasts, the size of quail eggs. My long legs were shown off to their best advantage sheathed in the finest of silk stockings, the tightest of breeches buttoned just below the knee. I had the hind end of a young boy and, as for that part of my anatomy that was decidedly lacking, an old pair of stockings knotted into a ball and tacked with a few stitches inside the crotch of the breeches added the necessary slight bulge.

Trinity's bells pealed the hour. The biggest wedding feast Newport had known in months was about to begin. I slipped into my coat, fastened the pewter buttons, adjusted my cravat, and placed the tricorn on top of my wig. One last look at the young man in the glass, and then down the stairs I bounded, a greeting to the innkeeper's wife, and out onto Thames Street, busy as always this Saturday, with oxcarts and carriages drawn by fine Narragansett-bred horses. No carriage for me, but the walk was a short one and I welcomed the opportunity to stretch my legs and catch a glimpse of *Andromeda*, tossing on the harbor chop and pulling at her dock lines like a restless filly.

The schooner *Andromeda* was more often my home than the drafty rented room above the Osprey Inn; I loved her as my own. That morning I assessed her exterior quickly, with a practiced and loving eye. Her reddish-brown sails were neatly furled on the booms, her rigging had been freshly tarred, and although her faded hull was in need of a coat of paint, it could wait until spring. Paint was dear. I inspected the dock lines for signs of chafing, making certain she was well before turning toward Spring Street, shoving my hands, red and cracked, deep into my coat pockets to warm them. The sun was bright, but the late October air was raw, smelling of tidewater and wood smoke from hundreds of chimneys.

As for my own wedding day, I couldn't even recall what the weather had been, foul or fair, but I remembered well my mood was gloomy and resigned. Ah, but Aeneas had been a good old man, a firm but kind husband for the brief time I was his wife. And I might have married again, to the man whose memory remained a burning ember, but no. The one man who had known me well, the man who had accepted my ruse but had loved the woman inside, that man was gone from my life. The sorrow over losing him, I still felt it; he was my first love, though I never could have lived as a warrant's wife, kept like a cat in dark, close quarters belowdecks on the very ship I once served as surgeon's mate. It wouldn't have worked, not for me. Not after who I had been and what I had done.

Sometimes in a reverie I imagined myself his woman—his wife—and it was good, it was enough. Sometimes I wondered if I had made a mistake, but it was too late to make amends. Some choices can't be undone. Perhaps most. Best not to think about it. Accept your fate: There will be no more weddings, no connubial rights, and no conjugal bliss for you, my dear. There'll be no brats with snotty noses who take after their papa. That life is not for you. You'll never be married except to the sea.

I was intimate with no one, I had no prospects for a match, but freedom—of that I had plenty. The freedom to do, to be, to pursue— and a livelihood too. As a man I could support myself, and more than that, I could invest, buy and sell property, take risks. Through my own hard work, I had acquired shares in the schooner *Andromeda* and her cargo—barrels and barrels of West Indian sugar, in the form of molasses, to be distilled into Rhode Island rum. Yankee gold. A fair number of Newport men had made their fortunes in this manner—why not Patrick MacPherson?

Just ahead stood the widow Redbone's house. Though made of Rhode Island timber, not stone, nor brick, the house was as fine as any in these colonies. Liveried servants waited at the gate to attend to horses and carriages. I had neither and walked straight up the steps and lifted the knocker, polished bronze, in the shape of an anchor. An African butler opened the door and took my hat with silent majesty, escorting me to a spacious parlor jammed with guests sumptuously dressed in the latest fashions from Paris and London. Ship owners, merchants, distillers, councilmen and their wives, many of whom I recognized though few of whom I had been formally introduced to. A relative newcomer to Newport was I, the groom's business partner, first mate at sea, and, when the occasion arose, a surgeon—a bleeder, a cupper, a puller of teeth, a setter of bones. The dull roar in the room, the rumbling house, the rising hum of conversation, was the sound of a receding wave raking a pebble beach. I experienced a moment of awkwardness, of near panic, as I looked about for a familiar face—someone I could converse comfortably with. Seeing no one I knew well or had been introduced to, I pretended to study a portrait on the wall.

For the most part I was comfortable passing as a man. I had been doing it for several years now, since I was eighteen; I had taken on the part. There was no male protector in my life, my father having died when I was sixteen and then my husband, Aeneas MacPherson, when I was but eighteen. It had been a brief marriage of convenience, lasting less than a year, during which time I assisted him in his duties as ship surgeon before he succumbed to the yellow fever. Aeneas left me his savings—all of it in silver—which now lay at the bottom of the ocean off the island of Nevis. After the shipwreck, I changed my name from Patricia to Patrick, taking the identity of a dead man—that of my late husband's nephew, a bona-fide surgeon's mate who had the misfortune to go down with his ship somewhere in the Indian Ocean during the last war. In the days to come I discovered Aeneas had left me something more valuable than a bag of silver—the ability to make my living by cupping, bleeding, pulling teeth, and setting bones. I became a surgeon's mate aboard the *Richmond*, whom I served during the victorious siege of Havana.

Becoming a man had done me well; it was almost second nature. I no longer had to think about how I stood, how I walked, or how I sat. My voice was low of its own accord, and scratchy; but speaking like a man, I had learned long ago, was more than just employing a lower register. There were many subtleties that distinguished male voice from female. Men tend to speak in bold, declarative sentences, I observed. No rise of inflection at the end of a phrase, no deference. Men don't drop their eyes. Men don't simper and they don't chatter. The most powerful men are comfortable with silence and can use it to their advantage. Yet, though I had mastered masculine mannerisms, the inner tension of knowing I wasn't who I pretended to be was always tightening my jaw and twisting my gut.

"Mr. MacPherson!"

I turned around at the familiar voice to see Everett Lee, the bridegroom's younger half-brother. At his side was a young woman in dove-gray silk with alert gray eyes—eyes that took me in and measured me with one shrewd glance.

"Patrick, I'd like to introduce Miss Mary Katherine Goddard, of Providence."

I knew the name Goddard; everyone in the colony knew it. Originally from New London, Connecticut, the Goddards had come to Rhode Island with a printing press to start Providence's first newspaper. Dr. Goddard had died; now only the Goddard women remained to run the print shop and publish the newspaper, the son William having recently left the colony to start a newspaper in Philadelphia. Everett had gone to work for the Goddards after returning from the siege of Havana, minus his right leg.

"I'm pleased to make your acquaintance, Miss Goddard," I said with Yankee straightforwardness, wondering if Everett was merely the young lady's escort or if he was indeed courting her.

An account of the wedding dinner would surely be printed in the Providence *Gazette* as well as Newport's *Mercury*, formerly published by Benjamin Franklin's brother James and then by James' wife, Ann. Colonial women were quite adept at continuing businesses their husbands had started, sometimes on their own, sometimes taking on a new partner, as the former Mrs. Redbone had done. The second marriage of a wealthy shipowner was of great interest to many. Although this bridegroom brought no family fortune to the marriage, Dominic Hale was highly regarded throughout the colony for his reliability as a shipmaster and for his shrewd head for business affairs. He was a hard man who spoke his mind and lived by his principles. He could be hell to live with, hot-tempered and unyielding, but he was honest.

"Have you heard about our recent bonfires, MacPherson?" Everett asked, nearly bursting with the news. "Newport isn't alone in her protests."

Of course, I had read about them; every coffeehouse in Newport subscribed to the *Gazette* as well as the *Mercury* and a dozen other colonial publications. The spark in his eyes and the expectant look on his face made me wonder if he had had more to do with the story than just printing it.

"Young mischief makers?" I said. "Or were our Sons of Liberty behind it?" It was common knowledge the Goddards were supportive of that not-so-secret society, active in Rhode Island and in every Northern colony.

"Why, Mr. MacPherson, how would I know? I'm only a compositor. I merely report the news," Everett said, unable to contain himself, fairly bursting with the fervor of the cause. That spark in his eye was a welcome sight to me—I didn't care if Everett himself had started the fire. He was a changed man from the bitter, forlorn adolescent whose gangrenous right leg I had amputated after it had been smashed by a cannon's recoil during the siege of Havana, three years earlier. He had confidence, and something else. Purpose, perhaps?

"I shouldn't think such pranks perpetrated by the local rabble will change the mind of Parliament, an ocean away," I said.

"Oh, it's not just the rabble, I assure you," Everett said. "There are bigger men behind it. Have you read Mr. Franklin's address to Parliament? You know there's a congress gathered in New York at this very moment, arguing what's to be done about the Stamp Act?" He was as animated as Dominic Hale on the matter—perhaps more so. Everett had little to lose and everything to gain, and because of that he had all the makings of a radical.

"Whether or not Parliament rescinds the act," Miss Goddard interjected, "I daresay there will be no man who ventures to enforce it in this colony. If they think there was trouble in Boston, they don't know Rhode Islanders."

"We certainly are a fractious, headstrong lot. I, for one, am glad to see Newport and Providence in agreement on something," I said. In truth, I knew little about the affairs of government.

"It's not just a local cause," Miss Goddard insisted. "Committee men in New Hampshire, Maryland, North Carolina—they're all planning a mock funeral on the first of November, the day the tax is to go into effect."

"A funeral?"

"For Liberty herself, Mr. MacPherson. We are being taxed against our consent, by a Parliament we have no voice in."

The impending tax would raise the cost of shipping. All bills of lading, invoices, and entry and export papers would have to be recorded on the official stamped paper purchased from the Crown in cash, which was notoriously scarce here. Coming on the heels of the revitalized Sugar Act, officially known as the American Revenue Act, and the empowerment of His Majesty's warships to search and seize our merchant ships, this was too much for us to bear. Us—I used the pronoun *us*, not *them*. Although I had been born in Barbados, raised in an English boarding school, and served aboard a British frigate, I had been making my living aboard a colonial schooner and frequenting Rhode Island coffeehouses for the past three years. I considered myself a Rhode Islander—a Newport man. And a contentious lot we were, up in arms about any issue that infringed upon our right to make a living in the manner we were accustomed to. It was the Yankee way.

"The stamp distributor has resigned, the governor has refused the oath, and the stamped papers have still not arrived," I said cheerfully. "Liberty is not yet dead, Miss Goddard. Let's not cast a pall on this wedding feast with talk of taxes and funerals."

"They are all that's certain in this world." Her smile was wry. "So says Mr. Franklin."

"Oh, we won't go down easy. There may be a funeral, but it won't be Liberty's—not here in Rhode Island," Everett quipped, unable to let the topic drop. "Mr. Howard only resigned his post as stamp distributor because he feared for his life. Having a straw man in your image tarred, feathered, and burned sends a message, does it not?"

"I admit it affects me greatly," Miss Goddard said. "This tax, if we acquiesced, would ruin the printing business. We simply won't comply. Riots, on the other hand, sell more papers. I'll take riots and bonfires any day."

Just then I spied John Eli, one of *Andromeda's* partners and former first mate, across the room; he was conversing with the host and hostess. "Look, there's Mr. Eli and his wife. Shall we join them in giving the newlyweds our joy?"

Everett's smile was a humorless twist of his lips. He had long nursed resentment toward Dominic, his older and more successful half-brother.

"Indeed, we shall, and wholeheartedly," said Miss Goddard, taking Everett by the arm. "Come, let us rejoice in your brother's good fortune."

"And the bride's," said I, defending my partner's reputation. "Mr. Hale is a fine catch. He will guard her fortune well, and grow it."

We crossed the crowded room, Everett stumping along on his wooden leg like a lugger sailing to windward, bearing the printer's daughter proudly on his arm, to take our places at the tail end of the queue of guests waiting to offer congratulations to Dominic and the new Mrs. Hale. They had been married in a private ceremony that same morning. Her gown, I noticed with a twinge of envy, was a lustrous yellow silk cut in the latest fashion and smacking of Paris. Her stern Yankee face, blade-nosed and thin-lipped, was decidedly softened by a stylish coif (again, in the French manner) and a bride's radiant smile. This young widow had been courted by half a dozen eligible bachelors and widowers, yet she had chosen my partner Dominic Hale, who was not a wealthy man but a successful man nonetheless. A demanding and ambitious man, I might add.

But today, their wedding day, they were both aglow with sentiment. Though it was a second marriage for both, and a convenient match, they seemed giddy as virgins, all blushes, smiles, and dewy eyes. I was glad to see Dominic so content, having seen him in in a perfect rage of grief after his first wife died, two years before. I hadn't liked him at first, quite the opposite.

I looked on as the two brothers greeted each other. Everett congratulated Dominic, bid joy to his new wife, and introduced Miss Goddard, who would write an account of the wedding feast for the *Gazette* that would include not only the guest list and menu but hint at some changes in the Redbone shipping firm to be implemented by Dominic Hale. And then it was my turn. I looked behind me to find I was last in the receiving line.

"Mrs. Hale," I said, making a knee and taking the bride's outstretched hand, gloved in fine Spanish kid. "Give you joy, madam. Every happiness."

"Thank you, Mr. MacPherson. Mr. Hale has spoken of you with high regard. He tells me you're a fine seaman as well as a medical man, a surgeon." She was gracious, if not exactly warm. She was strong, his equal—I sensed it immediately.

"I'm pleased to finally make your acquaintance," she continued. "I do hope we'll be entertaining you often."

"I am honored, madam." I caught her eyes briefly. She accepted me for who I said I was, without reservation. But I could also tell I wasn't important to her. She was just being polite.

Standing at her side, my partner beamed with pleasure. His normally obsidian eyes had gone as soft and moist as stewed prunes.

"My congratulations, sir." I extended my hand but Hale threw open his arms and, to my great surprise, embraced me, gruff as a bear.

"Patrick!" His voice was thick with emotion.

"Every joy, Dominic," I managed to say, as he squeezed the air from my lungs.

"Thank you. I can't believe my good fortune. Anna is a jewel and will be a good mother for Chauncey. The girl can now have a proper home and be brought up as a young lady should. I am a lucky man indeed." He now held me at arm's length, his fingers clasping my shoulders. "But what's this? Your hand is empty? We must fix that immediately." He raised his hand peremptorily, looking around for one of his wife's servants. Within seconds, it seemed, I held a large goblet of wedding punch. Rum, of course. The entire town had grown rich on it.

"To your health and happiness." I raised the glass to my lips. A good stiff punch it was, warming my throat and softening my brain. When his wife turned to speak to a servant, Hale pulled me aside.

"Before we sit down to dinner, I want to acquaint you with your first mate for the upcoming trip. His name is Cyrus Lovelace. Anna's cousin on her mother's side."

"My first mate?" I must have misunderstood, or perhaps he misspoke in his exuberance. For I was Dominic Hale's first mate and had been for nearly two years, ever since John Eli had taken a wife and inherited a sheep farm from his father.

Hale gripped my shoulder with his bear paw of a hand, his black eyes boring into mine. "I'm promoting you to shipmaster, Patrick. What do you say to that, *Captain* MacPherson?" He grinned like a madman and slapped me on the back, nearly spilling what was left of my punch. At the word "shipmaster" my heart did a strange little jig. I felt my jaw slacken. Looking into his face, I could think of nothing whatsoever to say. Was he jesting? Baiting me, perhaps?

"Lovelace grew up a waterman; he has sailed as mate on coasters; he has sailed on Redbone vessels. He knows these waters intimately. But he's young—younger even than you are, and a bit of a hothead, and still green when it comes to the nuances of trading. Patrick, you know how I carry out my affairs. Our affairs. You've made connections, you know *Andromeda* well—how she is to be laden, how to handle her in every condition. You know because I've taught you. I want you in command. I'm giving you Cyrus Lovelace and three men. A short crew, but you can do it; more profit for us with fewer mouths to feed and wages to pay. But you'll have to scramble to get everything in order and underway before the first of the month."

My head spun; my ears roared. "But—what—have you retired, sir?"

Dominic laughed and clapped me on the back again, but this time I was ready.

"Retired?" He roared. "I've never been more occupied. But just now I need to involve myself with my wife's fleet of vessels, all making ready to leave the harbor before the damned papers arrive. You too, Patrick, must oversee the preparations for our little venture and depart as soon as possible."

"But what about the livestock? Do we have sheep? Horses?" In addition to rum, which everyone carried, we specialized in animals on the hoof; we had modified our ship to accommodate them, having a ready market in the West Indies.

"None to be had—not until spring, Eli informs me. But I've bought up odds and ends, enough to fill her hold. A collection of cornmeal, candles, cobblestones, and rum. Plenty of rum. And the cobblestones cost us naught but the labor—ha!—they'll provide ballast on the voyage out. That was a brilliant suggestion on your part, Patrick." That Havana was actually buying cobblestones to pave her streets was too good an opportunity to pass up.

"When—"

"All to be delivered tomorrow. I've arranged for loading but you'll need to be on hand to oversee the manifest. You're to provision, obtain clearance papers, and set sail as soon as you possibly can. There won't be a ship left in the harbor come November when the stamped papers arrive. Though who will be idiot enough to enforce the tax here in Newport, I can't imagine."

"And what about returning?"

"The colony has formed a protest, and we're not alone. I'm betting that Parliament will come to their senses and rescind it when we refuse to comply. But there may be trouble. To be on the safe side, enter the bay by the light of the moon. Unload at John Eli's wharf. We'll have watermen freight the barrels to the warehouses, along with local produce."

I fairly reeled with the knowledge of my elevated status and the increase in my percentage of the profits it entailed. Not to mention the responsibility; I was to be in command. I was to be *Andromeda's* shipmaster, though only because Dominic would be too busy with his new responsibilities, the Redbones' fleet, brigs and ships built for transatlantic trade. That was the way of the world. One man advanced and another rose to fill his place. As for my instructions to slip in unseen on my return and off-load by moonlight like a common smuggler, I was willing to do it, if need be. My partners and the men of this colony would back me up, I felt certain.

"Thank you, captain. I relish the opportunity."

"Don't thank me until you've returned, and the sugar is safe in the warehouse, *Captain* MacPherson," he shot back, emphasizing the title in a manner that was meant to challenge me rather than flatter me. Then, pulling me close again in a brotherly fashion, he whispered hoarsely, "Patrick, I'll always be grateful to you for helping Marguerite in her last hours. And for your concern for Chauncey. We've disagreed on many things but you've become family." He clenched my shoulder and drew a deep breath.

Captain Hale's newfound happiness and fortune had made him both magnanimous and vulnerable. I pretended to examine my glass of punch, nearly empty though it was, giving him a few seconds to regain his composure, while I wondered where young Chauncey Hale was. Hiding on the stairway with her new siblings, spying on the adults? The girl had pulled at my heartstrings, stirred my maternal feelings, yet I could not act on them. To the seven-year-old girl I would always be Uncle Patrick. I hoped Hale's new wife would be a kind stepmother.

"Yet it's not for your concern nor for your surgical skills that I pass to you command of our swift little schooner. I trust you will make a quick and profitable trade for our shareholders, and a discreet return. You'll be sailing short-handed, standing your watch in turn, but you'll be paid a captain's wages in addition to your shares. As long as you're successful," he added.

"I understand the risks," I said.

"Of course you do. I taught you." Hale smiled. "Here's to your first run, MacPherson. To fair winds and fortune. The best of luck."

We touched our glasses and I tipped my head back, draining what was left of the punch, feeling on top of the spinning world.

Hale looked over my shoulder. "Here comes the governor. Stay by me and I'll introduce you to a very influential man."

A bewigged, white-gloved Black man announced dinner with the ringing of a bell—a bronze ship's bell—and opened the doors to the dining room. A banquet table, covered with Irish linen, was set with fine Dutch porcelain and locally crafted silverware. Rhode Island–made spermaceti candles burned in silver sconces—an extravagance, since it was midday and we had no need of light, yet they provided a warm ambiance of affluence. Thirty-two Chippendale-style chairs, made by our Newport craftsmen, Goddard and Townsend, fit easily around the long table—which was actually three tables placed end-to-end, I discovered, having unfortunately been seated at the crack.

Discreetly peering beneath the covered table, pretending to adjust my stocking, I saw they weren't proper tables but slabs of wood laid upon trestles. Yankees are practical and resourceful, even when making a spectacle. I smiled, feeling a flush of pride to be one of them.

Dominic sat at the head of the banquet, his new wife at the opposite end, with fifteen guests along either side. My partner was the very picture of a colonial merchant made good. At sea I was accustomed to seeing him in his serviceable canvas trousers, a coarse homespun shirt, and a Monmouth cap, but this afternoon he sported silken breeches and stockings, a linen shirt, and a brocade waistcoat set off by an exquisite stock, expertly knotted He wore his fine new coat well—like he was born for it. But no wig; Dominic never wore a wig. He tied his shock of hair with a grosgrain ribbon at the nape of his neck as if an afterthought. It was rather appealing, I thought. He was a handsome man, in a hard, rugged way. I might have fallen for him myself—in fact, I rather did—but I found it much more advantageous to be his partner in business. Dominic never would have appreciated me as a woman, I was certain.

I found it liberating here in these colonies, how a man can jump between the classes. None of these Yankees were true gentlemen, men of leisure, and certainly not titled. They worked hard for their wealth, those that had it. Those that didn't, believed they might— with any luck at all. Becoming wealthy was everyone's occupation in Newport, it seemed to me, and we all worked at it fanatically.

The new Mrs. Hale steered the conversation toward pleasantries and news—new wharves built, new babies born, new letters received from abroad—and the happy circumstances of those present. Decorum would not allow talk of ship seizures and the Stamp Act, not at the wedding feast, though it was on everyone's mind.

French Champagne served in Chinese porcelain cups paired with Narragansett oysters served on their own shells, sprinkled with salt from Tortola, and juiced with lemons from the Azores.

This delight was followed by courses of beef, lamb, pork, and fowl from the Narragansett plantations, each served with a different libation—Bordeaux, claret, cider, and Muscat—finishing with a

Yankee pudding and a lovely Sauternes.

Next came coffee, brandy, and cigars for the men. I was surprised to see the new Mrs. Hale and Miss Goddard remained in the dining room with us instead of joining the other ladies in the parlor. They kept silent, for the most part, but listened intently, Miss Goddard jotting down notes with a stub of a pencil. The men didn't seem to mind.

The afternoon became evening; a manservant added a log to the fire, sending a shower of red embers up the chimney. More candles were brought in, drinks refilled, and men got up to stretch and to relieve their bladders out back. I had not that luxury, so I curtailed my drinking and turned my attention to the conversation between two prominent merchants across the table. For several years now I had been listening to Dominic rail against Parliament's attempts to impose taxes on us, and I had heard the same talk in the coffeehouses of every colonial port I had visited. When I was struggling for my very existence in this world, the talk of taxation and duties had meant little, but gradually my situation had improved. I had worked hard as any man in the colony for what was mine. Now, as *Andromeda's* captain, I had even more to gain, and more to lose. I paid close attention to what the men were saying, noting its subversive bent.

Those in the room were all in agreement that it would be business as usual for us. The colony might be fiercely divided in local politics—the faction that backed Hopkins for governor versus the one that backed Ward—but when it came to taxes imposed on us by Parliament, we were all of one mind. We would ignore the Stamp.

We smoked our Havana cigars smugly, like lords, feeling united in our defiance and our growing sense of entitlement and outrage. One last round of toasts. I added my voice to theirs—*Hear him, hear him!*—took a mouthful of the brandy, savoring its smoky burn, my head and heart expanding while the voices around me swelled and crashed. I felt a part of something important. I was one of them, a Rhode Islander.

Two

All Saints Eve
Aboard the schooner Andromeda

A voyage to the West Indies from Newport this late in the year was always a gamble, yet for the moment luck seemed to be on our side. We sailed out of Narragansett Bay on a broad reach, the October air crisp and tart as a crab apple. I pulled my cap down low on my brow, squinting into the rising sun. The horizon was clear but a herd of wispy mares' tails high overhead foretold of a blow soon to follow.

A topsail schooner, *Andromeda* was not a large vessel—sixty-five feet on deck, nineteen feet wide at the broadest point of her beam, and drawing just seven feet of water, which was convenient when navigating the backwaters of Narragansett Bay. But she was well made, could carry a good deal of cargo when properly laden, and didn't require a large crew to sail. Her canvas sails were coated with herring oil and oak tannin, stiffening them for heavy-weather sailing and protecting them from the damaging effects of tropical sunlight and salt. The resulting coppery color made us nearly invisible on a moonless night—which might prove to be useful on our return.

Our decks were still cluttered with supplies delivered at the last hour; barrels and crates we would secure just as soon as we had the anchor cable stowed. On the foredeck, two of my men washed away the Narragansett mud with buckets of seawater before faking the thick hemp line into the cable locker. George, whose face seemed permanently twisted into a disfiguring scowl, was younger than he appeared. Twenty years old, he had been working on local fishing boats most of his life and could hand, reef, and steer better than I, without a doubt. The other man, Moses, was a Black Bermudian slave who worked as a carpenter in the Redbones' shipyard.

Moses and Sam, the African cook and deckhand, were the property of Dominic's wife, which meant they were in essence Dominic's property, acquired with his wife, her house, shipyard, and warehouses—all with an "I do" and a stroke of the pen.

Sam had thick white hair framing his wizened faced; bandy-legged, he walked with a limp but was agile and strong. I hoped he would be a frugal cook, making efficient use of our barely adequate vittles, in short supply this time of year.

I don't know how old Moses was; it was hard to judge. He might be twenty, he might be thirty. Hatless, he wore his hair plaited in a stubby queue made slick with grease. A scrap of faded red cloth tied around his forehead kept the sweat out of his eyes. Dark, unreadable eyes. His flaring nostrils indicated either determination or suppressed anger, I couldn't be sure. He seldom spoke except when spoken to. When he did, his English was perfectly understandable. Dominic assured me he was a good ship's carpenter, could hand and reef, and stand his watch as well as any.

Beside me, the blue-eyed Mr. Lovelace looked very much at ease with his hand lightly on the tiller, his feet comfortably apart, rocking with the ship's motion as effortlessly and as naturally as breathing. He exuded confidence and eagerness, a devil-may-care smile on his face like he was ready to take on whatever fate threw at him. I rather fancied him, I suppose.

Below, in the galley, Sam was singing as he prepared a sea pie for our midday meal, his voice carrying up on the wooden bones of the vessel, spilling into the wind. Was it a song from his African homeland? I could not make out the words; it was no song I had ever heard. Who were these men, my crew? I trusted them because Dominic did; he had handpicked them for me. And, I wondered, what did my crew think of me?

Soon we were past the point and into the sound, where fishing shallops and coastal traders were converging, all in a rush to get to port and unload before the stamped papers arrived and the tax went into effect. *If* it went into effect; many held out hope it would be repealed before it went into effect, but no news had come of that. What we'd find upon our return was anybody's guess. Homecoming was weeks away.

Home. I had long been in search of a port to call home, and Newport sufficed. Yes, this place suited me. We enjoyed a great deal of independence in this colony. Unlike other colonies, we elected our own governor, a privilege guaranteed under our charter. We were loyal to the King but scorned Parliament's duties. Called Rogue Islanders, smugglers, pirates, and worse, we cared not about our reputation but profited by it. I had a future in Newport—as a man, that is. Yet only at sea did I feel entirely comfortable with the strange creature I had become—a woman living as a man.

With the anchor now secure on deck and the cable properly stowed, George and Moses loosened the sheets to allow the sails to catch the wind, abaft the beam now, coaxing every bit of possible speed from the schooner. They worked in silence, for they both knew without words what needed to be done.

"She rides well," my first mate said, his face alight with pleasure, the wind twisting and toying with a stray wisp of his fair hair like a loose buntline. "No pull on the helm. She's well-trimmed, a pure joy to sail, sir."

I nodded, feeling warm inside, as if it were me he had praised. "You're right about that, Mr. Lovelace. Let us continue to make all due speed; with any luck, we can outrun the foul weather at our heels."

"Outrun it, we can. But what happens when we return? It could be tricky."

"That's why I have you along, Mr. Lovelace. Mr. Hale tells me you can navigate these waters blindfolded. He tells me you're the man to play chase with the King's men, and win."

"I am just the man for dodging revenue cutters," he said, flashing me a cocky grin. "I was one of the men impressed by the *Saint John* gang last year. Arrogant son of a bitch, that Lieutenant Hill. But we showed 'em, didn't we? Shot their mainmast off, didn't we? And with the governor's approval, at that. I relish a good chase, Captain."

Cyrus Lovelace had all the cheek of a Yankee, born and bred. He would speak his mind whether I asked his opinion or not. Was that because we were so close in age? Or was he challenging me, wanting to take my place?

We now left the Rhode Island Sound behind us, entering the open sea. The wind blew more forcefully, more steadily, and the deeper water here was a silvery gray color. We eased the sheets and picked up speed across the water, crashing into the rolling swells on a broad reach. The salt spray seemed to hang in midair for an instant, shimmering and sparkling in the sunlight, before raining down on the foredeck.

"Ease the fores'l," I called out to George. "Give her some rein!" He let out the line, the jib billowed, and the schooner settled into her stride.

Cyrus was grinning with the pure pleasure of being at the helm of a well-trimmed schooner making good speed on her voyage out. I took a deep breath and allowed myself a moment of satisfaction. There were forces beyond my control but at least I had a fine ship and a good crew. We'd be three weeks at sea, more or less. A week or two in Havana, and then home again.

There were unknowns, always unknowns. Would the situation in Havana be the same as last spring? Havana was technically no longer a free port as it was during the British occupation—it had been given back to the Spanish at the peace talks—but the local magistrates turned a blind eye. Rebuilding the wealthiest city in the Caribbean and enlarging the fortress required all manner of goods, and open trade benefited all the colonies—but Spain could bring down the hammer at any time.

On this run we carried New England cobblestones as ballast; stones to pave the city's new streets and squares. On top of the stones were hogsheads of Rhode Island rum, always in demand wherever there are soldiers and laborers. And on top of that had been stowed barrels of stone-ground flint corn, a few bundles of barrel staves, and Rhode Island–made spermaceti candles. Each man carried his own little adventure as well, to be traded or sold for his own personal gain.

Trading in Havana had been my inspiration and Dominic had not taken keenly to it at first. He generally did most of his business with the French island of Martinique, where his first wife had been born and raised. Most all of his connections were on Martinique and Guadeloupe; he had long traded with them — even during the war.

But courting the widow Redbone had expanded his imagination, and he had taken my suggestion to make a run to Havana, a run that had turned out most fortunate for us.

Besides molasses, Havana had what Rhode Islanders needed most, and that was hard currency—the universal currency—silver and gold. Money had always been in short supply in the northern colonies but the recent Currency Act that Parliament threw down really hit us hard. Havana, Spain's rendezvous port for its galleons laden with silver and gold from the Americas, was a bank of ready cash.

Late afternoon, the sun coloring the clouds a smoldering orange. *Andromeda* was settling into a rhythm. The watch was set and I was attempting to get to know my men. George had the helm for the second of the dog-watches. We weren't as regimented as the navy—we employed far fewer men and our objective was trade, not protection or capture—but like the navy we kept a four-hour watch schedule with a pair of two-hour watches in the late afternoon, which allowed us to rotate who had the midnight watch.

Cyrus Lovelace and I were belowdecks in the galley. Sam dished up our supper into the wooden trenchers we used as bowls. Stewed pork and apples and a loaf of country bread—the last fresh food we'd have for a couple of weeks. If we were lucky we'd pick up some fruit and vegetables in Havana, and perhaps a chicken and some fresh eggs. It was up to me to strike up a conversation, or to eat our meal in silence. I decided to be straightforward.

"Mr. Hale speaks highly of you. He told me you're Mrs. Hale's kinsman, is that right, Mr. Lovelace?"

My mate nodded, chewing his food with obvious enjoyment. "She and my mother are cousins."

"He tells me you grew up on ships."

Lovelace met my eyes and grinned. "My father had me cut out for a farmer. It was my mother who talked him into letting me apprentice with the Redbones. When I was twelve I shipped as Captain Redbone's personal servant. He took a shine to me. Taught me to navigate." He broke off a chunk of bread and dipped it in the trencher, mopping up the juice. "Next voyage he assigned me to work with the bosun. I learned how to mend sails and splice lines. Then when I was fourteen he put me to work in the shipyard. The next summer I worked in the warehouse, rolling hogsheads and lifting crates."

"A well-rounded education for a waterman," I said.

"When the Old Man found out I had a head for figures he showed me the bookkeeping side of the business. But I prefer to be on deck, not stuck behind a desk counting another man's money."

"Redbone had a heap of that." I chewed on a piece of pork, savoring the fat.

"But it did him no good, for all of that."

Redbone, I knew, had been wounded during the last days of the war when his cartel ship sailed into the French port of Saint Domingue under a flag of truce and was promptly seized by the *Cerberus*, a twenty-eighter. We all knew that few colonial flag-trucers carried prisoners of war for exchange, as they were commissioned, but instead were pretexts for trading with French colonies. I had also heard that Redbone managed to bribe his way out of the charges but a fortnight later he died. From blood poisoning, I had heard.

"Unfortunate, how he died. A man in his prime," I said.

"It was indeed a misfortune—for him." Cyrus looked up from his plate and gave me such a sunny smile it made my heart trip. "As for me, I don't intend to go that route."

"None of us do. We all intend to die valiantly for some greater purpose. Or peacefully, after a long and prosperous life. Tell me more about who you are. Your family. You mentioned a father and a mother. Are they alive? Do you have siblings, Mr. Lovelace?"

"My father lives; my mother has passed on. I have a brother and a sister, a twin sister. She's quite a beauty, if I do say so. You must meet her, captain. I hope to introduce you." His face revealed his intent. I was flattered, amused, and a little frightened to think of myself as an eligible bachelor, a good catch for someone's sister. If the Miss Lovelace had Cyrus's high, wide cheekbones, his hair the color of wheat, his sparkling blue eyes, and his spirit, she would indeed be attractive. My heart picked up its pace in spite of myself.

"I'd be delighted to meet your family, Mr. Lovelace. I have none of my own. I should love to have a sister. A brother." My voice trailed off; I said no more about my loneliness. "A drink with me, Mr. Lovelace?"

He grinned. "Delighted, sir."

I fetched a bottle of my own Madeira stored in a compartment under the deck and poured us two glasses.

"To families and fortunes." Which I wanted more was difficult to say.

My mate raised his glass. "To families and fortunes. Our fortunes," he added. We drank the fortified wine and I poured us another glass. The galley was still pleasantly warm from the iron stove. Around us the rushing of water against the hull, the creaking of the ship's old joints as she rose to meet each swell, the murmur of the men's voices above was familiar and comforting. It was dark now but no need to waste oil or candles; our eyes adjusted to the darkness. The darkness and the wine emboldened us and we talked with exaggerated confidence of our plans for the future.

"I must warn you, Mr. Lovelace, this isn't a brig like you're accustomed to working on, where every man has his assigned duties, his set watch. *Andromeda's* an undermanned little schooner racing with the thoroughbreds; we carry the scraps the big ships leave behind. Each of us aboard does twice the work of a jack on a big merchantman—it's the only way the ship can make a profit. That, and saving pennies everywhere we can. A fast voyage with little time spent in port."

"I'm your right-hand man, captain. I'm a jack of all trades; I can do everything that's to be done aboard a ship."

"And you follow orders?"

"Of course I follow orders. Every man answers to someone, do they not? A ship of any size can only have one man in charge."

"If I didn't know better, I'd say you were after my position," I said, baiting him with a laugh. We were developing an alliance, but an edgy one. I, myself, was still learning the fine art of striking a bargain. Successful trading was more than driving a hard bargain; it was developing a rapport with others, it was establishing trust and dependability. This was best done, I had learned from Dominic Hale, not through coercion but through goodwill. Eating and drinking with patrons and suppliers was one way to develop a bond, but the trick was not to drink too much or show any weakness. To be congenial but dominant.

If I could invest my modest earnings in other ships and their cargos I'd make more of a return while spreading my risk. A wise investor didn't put all of his eggs in one basket. Initially my goal was simply to get by, to earn a living. A good living, but why stop there? Why not a fortune? All around me in Newport men were making fortunes; why not me? But what I wanted more than a fortune was simply a place to call home. If that home was a floating one, well, that was all right by me. I knew I'd be wise to diversify, but I felt a developing sense of ownership for *Andromeda*. I suppose that was the woman in me, wanting a home. *The next thing you know you'll be hanging chintz over the portlights and churning butter in the galley*, I chided myself.

Together we finished the bottle, growing accustomed to one another's presence, venturing beyond boasting and bravado. I asked him again about his family; he told me more about his father and his sister, his only living relatives. Which was two more than I had.

"Juliana has a sharp wit. And she's very fair. I hope you meet her; you'd make a good couple. The Captain and Mrs. MacPherson. Then we'd be brothers, you and me." He laughed and I forced a chuckle.

"I'm in no position yet to wed, though it would be my pleasure to meet your family. But you, Mr. Lovelace, have you designs on any of the young Newport beauties?"

"I rather have my eye on Mr. Keen's daughter."

"Keen, the distiller?"

"Yes. His daughter Cassie is very fine. Quite beautiful, though sharp of tongue."

I felt the wash of disappointment, knowing beauty was what men most treasured in women. A pleasing face, a well-formed figure. I had neither.

"The problem is, I also have feelings for Miss Tucker. I've known her since we were this high. Our families expect us to marry, and I think Miss Tucker does too. But I'm not ready for all of that."

"Such a dilemma, eh? But you're right; you're in no position yet to wed."

He sighed—a sigh of relief. "Is it true what they say about the

West Indian women?"

"I wouldn't know." I felt my face flush. "I'm a temperate man."

"Well, I mean to find out. I aim to discover for myself if they're as good as they say."

"There will scarcely be time for frolic, Mr. Lovelace. Keep in mind I have no mercury aboard to dose you with, so I'd advise you to abstain," I said, ending the conversation. I then rose, stretched, and bid him goodnight. A captain can't afford to be too familiar with anyone on board—least of all, a captain with something to hide.

Mr. Lovelace went to his berth and I to mine to catch a few hours of sleep. Sam slept too, in his hammock strung up in the galley by the warmth of the stove; I could hear his snores. While on deck George kept a steady course and Moses kept a lookout as *Andromeda* rode through the dark sea.

Ten days out of Newport and the wind began to shift, portending a change in the weather. Sure enough, the next day the wind set in strongly from the north. I wanted to ride that wind for all it was worth, hoping it would take us quickly south. With all luck on our side, we'd outrun the storm that was brewing.

The men knew it was coming as well as I did, and possibly better. We finished our cornmeal mush quickly, the sound of spoons scraping wooden bowls, and drained the last of Sam's bitter, burned coffee. Then we spent the morning making certain everything aboard was stowed properly and securely lashed down. Sam cooked up enough johnnycakes to last three days and brewed three gallons of sugared coffee to be drunk cold in case rough seas prevented lighting the galley stove.

Mr. Lovelace heaved the log and George counted the knots that slipped through his hands, while I watched the sand run through the tiny minute glass. We were making seven knots—top speed for *Andromeda*. I took the noon sight just as clouds gathered on the horizon. The wind picked up through the afternoon, driving the sea into froth and filling the air with spume. Hatches battened down, sails reefed, we sailed south by southeast. And then the wind backed and the rains came, slashing at us, stinging like pellets as the sea rose into mountainous peaks, lifting us up and bearing us along. We took turns at the helm, hands firm on the tiller, to keep from broaching. Sam sang when he took his turn, his voice rich and deep as a cello contrasting with what sounded like a violin screeching high aloft.

Andromeda raced along on a scrap of a staysail, plunging down the steepening slopes, ever in danger of burying her bowsprit in the troughs. We had to slow our speed, had to stay on the backside of the peaks rather than be pushed down the front and pitch-poling, nose over heels, to our doom.

"George, Moses, rig us a sea anchor, if you please." I had to shout, cupping my hands around my mouth to be heard. The men lurched to the lazaretto, bending low as a deluge of water swept over the rail and across the deck, swirling around our legs in its mad rush to return to the sea.

We saw no more of the sun that day. No lanterns could be lit, in case of a knockdown. We took our turns standing watch, steering by the feel of the wind on our face and the force of the water against the rudder. All around us, a deafening sound—the snarl, hiss, and roar of the ocean overlaid with the furious screaming of the wind in the rigging. Belowdecks, it was worse. Belowdecks I could hear every crack and groan of the ship's bones as she flexed under the sea's weight. I prayed she would not founder. Try as I might I could not sleep but lay wide awake in the blackness, wedged into my bunk, bracing myself against the jarring movements, trying to make sense of the din while waiting for the knock at my cabin door.

I had just fallen into oblivion when it came. "Captain!"

"Aye, Mr. Lovelace, I'm coming." I tumbled to the floor and pulled on my coat and hat. It was midnight and my turn on watch along with George, who was already on deck and eager for the task. A nod of thanks to Sam and Lovelace, dripping wet and exhausted as they stumbled below.

I turned the sand glass on its gimbals mounted on the binnacle.

George's bare hands on the tiller, moving easily, rhythmically, like he was working a weaver's loom or a printing press. The trick was not to fight the tiller but to work with the powerful force against the rudder. Each enormous wall of water rising behind us presented a test of skill and luck, a seemingly endless succession of life-or-death chances dealt out by God or the Devil, I knew not. With our makeshift sea anchor—a tangle of knotted hemp and canvas buckets dragging off the stern to slow our speed, and a staysail for stability, I hoped we could ride out the gales.

The night was so dark, so pitch black, I couldn't see the foremast from the helm. All a roar, the wind screaming in the rigging, the snarl and roar of running seas; I had to shout for George to hear me and he was standing beside me. The ship could weather this, as long as we didn't get beam end to the seas. As long as we didn't pitch pole, head over heels. As long as we didn't take on too much water. These are things never spoken aloud aboard ship but never out of mind.

The minutes dragged by. Hours. Still, the pounding and the roar, unrelenting. The ever-present danger. Nothing to do but endure.

I turned the sand glass and relieved George, settling in for my turn steering. The rudder felt like a demon had it in its teeth; it took both hands to steer. This is just a gale, I told myself. Nothing but a hard blow. *Trust your ship, captain.*

And then it blew harder. The wind's scream rose in pitch, a crazed opera soprano, and the wall of water behind us steepened, blowing a constant spray of icy water on our backs. George stood to windward of me, swaying like a young tree, his feet spread, one knee wedged against the binnacle. He stood as if in a trance.

There was no warning for what came next. Out of the darkness an enormous cross swell hit us on the beam with a crack and cascaded over the rail, knocking me down, covering me with a flood of icy water and carrying me away. I grabbed for the rail and clung to it as the ship fell to starboard, her deck perpendicular to the sea. She shuddered as she strove valiantly to right herself like a fallen horse struggling to get back on its feet.

God, I loved her at that moment even as I was covered with seawater, holding on for my life. It passed through my mind, the realization of what a fine ship she was, and my crew, the best men ever. I lost one grip, then the other, swept away toward my doom. Lungs bursting, grasping for a handhold, mad to breathe, wanting air, losing consciousness... Something—someone's hand—grabbing me, saving me, pulling me like a rag doll up over the rail and onto the deck, where I collapsed—gagging, choking, gasping, breathing again at last as seawater poured across the deck, emptying through the scuppers in its mad rush to return to the source.

Regaining my senses, I looked up to see Cyrus Lovelace standing over me, dripping wet and beautiful as a young Neptune.

"Hell's teeth!" I roared, spitting seawater. "How did you—?"

Cyrus gave me a hand up, bracing me as I struggled to regain my balance. "Nearly my watch," he yelled, making himself heard over the wind. "I'll take the helm now. Moses will be up shortly to relieve George." He set about lashing himself to the binnacle with a length of rope, a precaution I should have taken.

I gripped his shoulder in acknowledgment. "You saved my life, Cyrus." First names between us seemed to be in order now, but the mate shook his head, embarrassed by the acknowledgment. Men aboard ships don't like to speak about the ever-present possibility of drowning, nor do they like the burden of being made into heroes.

"It was nothing."

"Thank you, just the same."

He made a fist with his thumb skyward.

"Keep the seas on the quarter," I said, going below.

In the privacy of my cabin I huddled beneath the damp, salty blanket, longing for the release that tears would bring, but I was unable to shed a single one. Unlike the men, I was all too willing to consider my own death by drowning, which I had narrowly just escaped because of the quick actions of my first mate. Even then, the ship might have not recovered had George not maintained control of the helm. Ifs, buts, because ofs—life seemed so precarious, so dependent on a great many variables all of which must be in alignment, that it seemed a miracle any of us survived. We were all guardian angels—safekeepers for each other.

Above, the storm still raged, the ship lurching like a drunkard leaving a pothouse, but remaining upright. Sam was at the pumps; I could hear them creaking. Just a few minutes to warm up, I thought, still shivering. Just a few more minutes... I fell into a most profound sleep.

Morning broke. I awoke to the banging of pots in the galley and the smell of Sam's coffee brewing. Dressing in my only set of dry clothes, I went on deck. Sodden gray skies overhead; the sun was a swollen red eye peeking out over a bruised horizon. The men had run up the foresail but the wind had dropped to almost nothing, sighing fitfully like a moody lover. The swell slapped against our hull from three different directions. Cyrus and Moses were inspecting the ship for damage. We had not come through unscathed.

"What's the matter?"

"Rudder loose," said Moses.

"Good Christ, when did this happen?" My voice sounded harsh as a seagull's. "Will she steer at all?"

"She's been hard to steer ever since the knockdown," Cyrus said. "A pintle might have worked itself lose. Then a big cross swell hit just before sunrise, and since then it's been very techy."

"Why didn't you wake me?"

He shrugged. "Nothing you could have done. We lost our wind; we weren't making any way."

I took hold of the tiller, moving it carefully to starboard and then to port. It felt like something was loose and the ship barely responded. Of course, without wind, it was hard to tell for certain. We couldn't chance losing our steering, yet to repair a rudder at sea was nearly impossible. There were other ways to alter our course— we could steer to some degree by the sails alone or by dragging something over the side—but without a rudder, making Havana was out of the question.

"We can't wallow here, drifting with the current. Now who will go overboard and have a look at it?"

"I will," Moses volunteered, to every other man's relief.

We dropped the foresail and were under bare poles, going nowhere, rolling on sloppy seas. George fetched a dock line while Moses stripped down, leaving his clothes in a heap on the deck. He tied one end around his waist, secured the other end around the taffrail, and then dove off the stern, disappearing under the vessel with a kick of his strong legs. We could see his dark shape moving beneath the water as *Andromeda* rolled from side to side on the swell. After about a minute Moses surfaced, blowing like a dolphin, and pulled himself up by the rope, his dripping body sparkling in the weak morning sun.

"Well? What did you find?"

"One pintle bent, one missing." He paused to catch his breath. "And the rudder cracked, captain. Split nearly in two."

"Can you stabilize it? Keep it intact until we make landfall?" We had a spare rudder below in the carpenter's storeroom but we'd need the shallow, protected waters of a harbor to replace it.

"Maybe bind it with tarred rope. Maybe help." He didn't seem assured but there was nothing to be lost by trying to save it.

"Do so. Do whatever you can. If this wind stays steady and if we can keep this course we'll raise the Virgins. George, assist Mr. Lovelace with inspecting our cargo. Make certain all is well balanced and secure. After Moses does what he can to stabilize the rudder, we'll trim our sails for optimal steering, to reduce the strain on it. We'll head for the nearest harbor for repairs. Christiansted harbor."

According to my deduced navigation, the Danish island was about two hundred miles to the southwest—just a few days away, if the winds picked up. There near the shore we could careen the ship or at least launch a platform for repairing or replacing the rudder.

As the sun rose it warmed the air and burned the clouds off. Soon we had a steady breeze. With the rudder jury-rigged in place and the sails set and perfectly trimmed, I set a course for Christiansted.

Three

Christiansted, St. Croix

The wind had dropped to barely a whisper, teasing and flirting with the sails, making us work the sheets to keep them filled. Every man was on deck; I was at the tiller, coaxing the crippled rudder as we ghosted into the outer reaches of Christiansted harbor, to anchor on the lee of Protestant Island. Here, the wind died altogether. Launching the ship's boat, George and Moses towed the schooner to set the anchor in the rich, black mud beneath us.

I breathed easier now that we were at anchor, safe for the moment in this shallow, sheltered bay. As captain of the ship I had to check in immediately with the Danish port officials and explain to them we were just here for emergency repairs, not to trade. We'd still have to pay a harbor fee, but with any luck we'd be on our way in a day or two. The men launched a floating platform and Moses was already overboard, removing the rudder. I took the damaged pintle ashore with me to have it repaired or a new one made.

After obtaining clearance I intended to look up my old friend Rachel Lavine, whom I'd met on Nevis some years ago when she was living under the protection of a Mr. Hamilton. The last I had heard from her she was moving to Saint Croix with her man and their two boys.

It was Rachel who had discovered me washed up on the beach outside her home after the hospital ship I was serving in hit the reef and went down. It was Rachel who rescued me, sheltering me when I had nowhere to go. It was Rachel who gave me her own bed, nourished me back to health, combed the tangles from my hair. We became close as sisters in just a few weeks' time.

And it was Rachel who helped me carry off my new identity, once I had set my mind to it. She lent me Mr. Hamilton's clothes— he was away at sea then. I had never returned them, had worn them out, in fact. If I should find her here in Christiansted, I would try to compensate her in some small way. Mostly, I just wanted to see her again.

Sam rowed me to shore, making for the wharf in front of the customs house. As we approached, my spirits rose unaccountably, as if I were discovering a new land. This colony, once French but sold to the Danes before I was born—was it a special place or was it just another ravaged, plundered sugar isle owned by a few wealthy planters? There were so many sugar isles in these latitudes and every one built on the backs of slaves and indentured servants. I was a child of sugar. My father had been a Barbadian plantation owner—my mother, one of his indentured servants. He had owned slaves from Africa, too—he had consorted with them, begotten children with them. As much as I loathed my past, I couldn't escape it; the profits from sugar sustained me even now.

Sam left me at the wharf to return to the schooner; I would hire a boat to return. I looked forward to the afternoon on shore, leaving *Andromeda* in Cyrus's able hands. After dealing with the authorities I'd stop at a tavern to slake my thirst and then find Rachel—if she was here in Christiansted.

After two weeks aboard ship, walking on terra firma felt

unnatural; my head seemed to swirl and my ears roared with the sound of the wind and the sea. I swayed with the lurching gait peculiar to seamen who have become accustomed to walking across a constantly shifting deck. Making my way along the waterfront, I took in the view of the Danish town. The old fort, the new warehouses, the customs house, all built of yellow brick. The streets were wide and straight, covered with a fresh layer of crushed coral and limestone that crunched underfoot. All order and progress, not a thatched roof or a dilapidated building to be seen. To the customs house, ship's papers tucked under my arm, weaving my way through a throng of hucksters, fishmongers, errand boys, and militia men, stepping aside for the Blacks rolling hogsheads of molasses to the docks. A chatter of patois I couldn't understand; the coarse blend of French, English, Danish, and a dozen African languages sounded like a great flock of starlings. Children of all shades, black, brown, and tan, chasing chickens and herding goats through the streets, swatting them with green sticks, shrieking at them like lieutenants. Women with dark, shiny, imperturbable faces gliding along carrying baskets of laundry to the beach to be bleached in the sun. Barefoot beneath their brightly colored skirts, yet imperious as Bantu queens. I felt a sudden and inexplicable longing for my childhood home.

Presenting my papers to the Danish official, I was granted permission to stay long enough to make repairs. My papers officially stamped, I proceeded to the harbor master's office to pay my anchorage fee, then made for a nearby tavern where I inquired about the Scotsman Hamilton and his family. The Creole proprietor gave me a strange look as he poured my ale.

"Is it Hamilton or his mistress you're inquiring about?"

"I'm a kinsman of Mrs. Hamilton," I said, which wasn't true, but we were siblings of a sort.

"Ah, yes. She has innumerable brothers and cousins." The proprietor's smile was conspiratorial and I understood the implication. "You'll find her quite easily, I'm certain. Company Street, number 34. Faucette Dry Goods, that's her other business."

I downed my beer quickly to quench my thirst, paid for it, and went back into the dazzling afternoon, my head pounding. Would she recognize me?

I found Company Street and Faucette Dry Goods quite easily. Faucette had been Rachel's maiden name, I recalled. Before Hamilton. Before Lavien. I entered the shop expectantly, the bell on the door tinkling as I opened it.

"Hullo?"

"Good afternoon, sir. How may I help you?"

I couldn't see her—my eyes had not yet adjusted to the dark interior—but her voice I remembered well. The French Creole accent, the musical inflection. Her voice reminded me of a woodwind instrument, distinctively mellow as an *haut bois*.

"Rachel." Her name burst from my mouth.

She moved from behind the counter in a rustle of taffeta. I smelled her before I could clearly see her face.

"Do I know you? Have we been introduced? Tell me, sir, what is your name?"

"Ah, what good are surnames, madame? They are never our own."

Yes, it was Rachel; I had clearly caught her off guard.

"That was what I said when you first asked me my name," I continued. "On Nevis. After you rescued me, a castaway, washed up on the beach. You took me in and nourished me. Dressed me in your husband's clothes."

"Patricia?" She came out from behind the counter to get a better look. "Is it really you?"

A laugh escaped me. "It's really me, yes! But please, call me Patrick. It was you who helped me change from Patricia to Patrick. Patrick MacPherson." I removed my hat and made a flourishing little bow. "I kept my late husband's surname. It was legally mine, after all."

Her hand, a white tern, fluttered to her décolletage. Her lovely décolletage. "What a joy! Can it be?" She approached me, her dark eyes wide, taking me in, enveloping me in a sisterly embrace. We both laughed, tears in our eyes.

"Here, let me have a look at you." She held me at arm's length to examine me, her dark eyes bright with curiosity and concern, before drawing me close again, more fiercely this time, her slender fingers pressing into my back.

"Oh, Patricia!"

I could feel her heart beating against my own, a reckless drumming, I could smell her own particular scent, breathed it in deeply, remembering all at once her odor, a blend of warm milk, irises, and the oil from her hair, gone silver at the temples.

"But what brings you here to Christiansted? Why on earth didn't you write and tell me you were coming? I suppose you didn't—but how did you find me? And how do you fare? Does a man's life suit you?" Her lilting voice, her laugh, bright as the tinkling bell over the door, lit up her face—a face beginning to show its age by the fine lines at the corners of her dark eyes and around her mouth, like delicate parentheses, an expressive face.

"You're as beautiful as ever, Rachel."

"And you, sir, are..." She held me again at arm's length to study me. "You are absolutely original."

I laughed out loud, but was dangerously close to tears.

"But do tell," she said, "what brings you here? I cannot believe my good fortune."

Where to begin? "I'm a shipmaster, can you believe it? Part owner of a trading schooner out of Newport, Rhode Island." It all sounded quite unbelievable as I spoke it aloud.

"A shipmaster? Why, I thought you were a medical man, a ship surgeon. Really? You change your identity with the wind, sir." She flashed me her loveliest smile and clasped my rough, red hands in hers.

"Ah, but there was little profit in bleeding and cupping. Fewer bones to be sawed, with the war over and the treaty signed. Newport is filled with medical men, besides. Filled with merchants too, but the trading business is profitable. Risky, but profitable. And you, Rachel, are you minding Mr. Hamilton's store?"

Her face clouded; the furrow between her eyes deepened, and

then vanished in a proud smile. "Mr. Hamilton has little to do with this store. It is my own endeavor. I will tell you the details over supper and you must tell me about your adventures. You will stay for supper, won't you?"

"I'd like nothing better, but I must see to my vessel. We've damaged our rudder and are here in port just long enough to repair it. Perhaps you could recommend a blacksmith? I need some pintles forged." I wanted very much to stay for the evening. I missed female companionship—Rachel's in particular. She and I had developed a close rapport during those weeks I stayed under her roof.

"I can get you your pintle made, and for a very good price. Lars Boesgaard, who owns the forge and employs two smiths, is a good friend of mine. I'll write you a note of introduction." She went to her desk and wrote a few words on the back of a calling card. "Give him this. You'll find his shop on the waterfront opposite the quay."

"I hate to leave so soon, but—"

"Go take care of your ship, but do come back and join us this evening, Alexander will be so pleased to see you again—and you'll meet James. We have so much to catch up on, so much to say to one another. Please do say you'll sup with us and stay the night."

The bell above the door rang as a customer entered—an older gentleman who greeted her in accented English. Tipping my hat, I bid Rachel a good afternoon and stepped out into the street.

It was now late afternoon. A stop at the forge to have a set of pintles made, leaving the damaged one to be repaired for a spare, and then back to *Andromeda* where the men had the new rudder nearly ready to mount. I gave them the night off aboard ship while I returned to shore to enjoy some female companionship.

Close around Rachel's table, the heat from the pepperpot and the red wine flushing our faces, an evening *en famille*. My head swam pleasantly, and I felt at home listening to her children recite their lessons. Their mother was eager to show me what good students James and Alexander had become.

"James starts his apprenticeship in a few weeks. He's to learn carpentry."

"An excellent trade, James. Always in demand. My carpenter is installing a new rudder, one he made himself, to replace the one that broke during the storm."

"Tell us about your ship," his younger brother asked. Alexander had grown a great deal since I had first seen him, a child of five, on Nevis. It had been, what, three years?

"She's a tops'l schooner," I said, pleased to talk about my vessel.

"What do you carry?"

"Whatever we can fill our hold with." I smiled. "We're Newport's scavengers, cleaning out what's left in the warehouses after the big brigs leave port. But it's a living. This voyage we have corn meal, cobblestones, candles, and rum."

"Rum to the Caribees? Isn't that like shipping coals to Newcastle?"

A precocious lad, that one. I looked to Rachel and winked. "It would seem so, Alexander. But actually there's a great demand for our rum. Spain is rebuilding her fort in Havana, an enormous task that requires thousands of men—soldiers, slaves, engineers, artisans. Hardworking, thirsty men. Cuba doesn't produce enough rum to quench a thirst that great. Right now our Newport rum fetches a good price in Havana, along with our other goods. But the opportunity won't last forever. The world is changing rapidly."

"Perhaps." Rachel's smile was wry and wistful. "But it's not changing fast enough for me."

"I remember you." Alexander stared at me, his eyes so unveiled, so guileless, I could practically see inside his mind. "You stayed with us when you were shipwrecked. Mother and I dragged you up from the shore. I remember you read to me, you read *Robinson Crusoe* and you doctored my foot when it was cut. But I was little then and I thought you were a woman when we found you on the beach." He blushed, suddenly embarrassed.

James laughed behind his hand.

"Alexander!" His mother reprimanded. "Where are your

manners? It's not polite to comment on such things. And you, James—you know better than to laugh at your little brother, which further embarrasses our guest."

I was blushing at the candid remark but there was no use to deny it. "You have a keen memory, Alexander. What are you now, eight years old?"

"Nearly nine, sir."

"You're quite right. A valid observation. You see, I was a woman when you and your mother found me washed up on shore." Then I lowered my voice and took on a conspiratorial tone. "I still am a woman. But I live as if I were a man." It sounded absurd saying it aloud.

"You pretend to be a man? Like, a masquerade?" He was trying to make sense of it.

"Rather like that, yes." I took a drink of wine, still looking at him over the rim of the glass.

"But why, sir?"

James, red-faced and smirking, stared hard at his plate.

"Why do I pretend to be a man?"

The young one nodded.

I sighed. How to sum it all up, what my life had become? "Because it suits me. It's how I get by. I was young, my husband died, I had no means of support. My father was dead, I had no brothers, no uncles—no one to take me in. I had to provide for myself; had to make my own living." I shrugged. "I have to get by somehow." What more was there to say?

Alexander nodded. "Like mother. She has to get by." He picked up his spoon and resumed eating. Rachel and I exchanged freighted glances.

"Yes, in a sense. Your mother and I are very much alike, though I have no children to care for and look after. Your mother is a very brave woman, and more resourceful than I am. For me, well, it's just that breeches are more convenient than skirts." I forced a smile, trying to make light of it. "Some qualities, like bravery or kindness, aren't the sole province of one sex or the other. Do you agree?"

The boy shrugged. "What then makes us different—men and women?"

James snorted with the superior knowledge of an older brother. His hands in his lap, he furtively pointing to his crotch, leering at his brother.

To which Alexander delivered a retaliatory kick under the table.

"That's quite enough!" Rachael said, taking control once again. "You boys will please clear the table and attend to your studies. Captain MacPherson and I are going out for walk."

"How is it that you're a shipmaster these days, not a ship surgeon?"

We strolled down to the waterfront, enjoying the cool evening breeze coming down from the hills. I loosened the knot of my stock to feel the air on my throat while Rachel pulled her shawl closer.

"It's a long story, madam. Suffice it to say, I'm an opportunist."

"I'm an opportunist as well, Patricia. We're both adventurers of a sort."

Away from her sons the cheerful mask dropped away, and the lilting voice flattened. I tried to lift her spirits, to make her smile.

"What will people think, a strange man coming to dinner and then escorting you out for a stroll after dark?"

Her laughter had a discordant edge. "I have little to lose. People think the worst of me as it is. My only goal in life is to make a better life for my sons."

"Every mother's goal, I'm sure. But what of Mr. Hamilton? When do you expect him to return?" I recalled that the adventurous Scot was often away for long periods of time.

"It seems he has sailed out of our lives forever."

"What? But you were to be married, here on Saint Croix. When I saw you last on Nevis, you told me so yourself. What happened?"

"The Church forbade my remarriage. Lavien remarried, yet I was denied that right. It seems I can never remarry. And the money I inherited is long gone."

"How do you manage?"

"Well enough." A slight shrug of her slim shoulders. "I've learned what men want and what they're willing to pay to possess it. I've learned how to calculate the market value of necessities, of luxuries. And what men will pay for the privilege of obtaining certain services."

The bitter irony in her voice wasn't lost on me; I had a feeling she wasn't just talking about selling dry goods. If so, she wouldn't be the first woman to give herself to a man she didn't love, nor would she be the first woman to run a discreet bedroom business, as mantua makers and milliners were rumored to do. Pamela and the forbidden Fanny Hill of Richardson's and Cleland's fervid imaginations came to mind—yet these were caricatures of fictional women invented by men—stories to be sold for their own profit. What stories would women themselves tell?

We approached the waterfront, walking past the warehouses, the taverns, and the marketplace, deserted at this hour.

"I should love some fresh produce," I said. "But tomorrow is Sunday and I won't be able to stay a day longer than is necessary to repair my rudder."

"I have some oranges and an abundance of pineapple I shall send you with."

I thought how young Chauncey Hale and her new siblings might enjoy the tropical fruit. I would save some to take back to Newport—we should arrive just in time for Christmas festivities.

Ahead, three watermen stumbled toward us, exuberant in their liquor and oblivious to our presence. Out in the harbor a hundred lanterns winked, their light dancing on the dark water. The restless sound of rattling blocks and slapping halyards made me restless to leave.

The old stone fort was a looming black shape just ahead. A sentry leaned against the wall, waiting for his watch to be over. Rachel stopped abruptly; I felt her stiffen.

"What is it? What's the matter?"

"Here. It was here I was jailed."

"Where? You were imprisoned at the fort? Surely not."

"He branded me a harlot. He was desperate to punish me, to make me one."

"You were very brave to come back to Christiansted."

She started to walk again, pulling me by the hand impatiently. The fort growing closer, looming ahead like a stone castle. I thought of the prisoners inside. Thieves and cutpurses. Murderers.

"Nothing has changed. I am still a fallen woman, my reputation beyond repair. The women refuse to speak to me or acknowledge my presence. Only the fishmongers and charwomen bid me good day. The men? They're far more forgiving. As a merchant, I'm successful, I suppose. The men of Christiansted are quite willing to do business with me. One man in particular, whom I count on as my good friend. Mr. Stevenson has ties with New York. I should like to go to New York one day..."

"Come with me, then. I'll take you to New York. You can make a new start."

Her laugh was a sharp, tinkling sound, like glass breaking. "I cannot. Now is not the time."

"Now is never the time," I said.

Rachel shivered. I put my arm around her slim shoulders, drawing her close. But she resisted me, pulling away, preferring to be alone in her bitterness. Rachel wasn't seeking my consolation, nor my answers; I had nothing to give her but my friendship.

"For three months and seven days I was held there, behind bars, in a most deplorable state. And the guards—" Her voice broke off. She gasped a ragged breath and continued. "They bound and gagged me so no one could hear my rage against them. They had their sport with me; they made certain I was a ruined woman."

"Oh, my dear Rachel..."

Her thin nostrils flared as she drew a breath and sighed. When she spoke again it was with quiet resolve. "It doesn't matter now about my reputation; it's too late for me. But I have James and Alexander to consider. They're old enough to hear the talk around town and to feel humiliation. Old enough to question."

"Are they Mr. Hamilton's children?" I blurted out.

"We live as man and wife; James claims my sons as his own, he always has. And he sends funds when he can but he's not a dependable means of support, he never has been. That man gets by on dreams and schemes, but he took me in and protected me when I fled from Lavien, and I shall always be grateful to him for that. He has a heart, James Hamilton. But his heart, like the rest of him, is never at home."

"His store, is it profitable? He provides for you in that way, does he not?"

"I told you, the store is my own venture entirely. Mr. Hamilton has nothing to do with it. A friend lent me the capital to start it. My sister's husband pays the rent—at least for the time being. The store supports us, more or less. But I want a better life for my sons. Next year Alexander will apprentice as a clerk under Mr. Stevenson's roof. Alex has an inquisitive mind—he's good with figures, have you noticed? And he's very close to the Stevenson lad—the two are fast friends, as close as brothers." She gave me a quick, meaningful look but I did not pursue the insinuation. Did Mr. Hamilton know, I wondered? Did the whole town, the whole island know?

We had walked past the fort now and from where we stood, we had a good view of the bay, shimmering under the starlight. Dozens of vessels facing into the breeze, tugging at their anchors, tearing at their bits, eager to run on the wind. I felt affection and pride for my ship, seeing *Andromeda* in this foreign port. A most seaworthy vessel, having brought us through the storm.

She was dark now, all lights extinguished. There would be a man on deck keeping an anchor watch; it would be Cyrus, at this hour, I knew, having set the watch schedule. He would be looking out across the bay, alert for any wind change, any small boat approaching. He carried a pistol and would not hesitate to defend us, though Christiansted seemed to be an orderly Danish town. The other men would likely be sleeping, perhaps on deck because of the heat. In any case, a well-deserved rest after the rough crossing and the rudder repair.

"See my ship out there?" I tugged on her sleeve, pointing out to the harbor. "See the schooner, the two-masted ship just off Protestant Cay? That's my *Andromeda*."

Rachel followed my outstretched arm, trying to pick out my ship from the dozens in the harbor. "She looks rather small from here."

"Yes, but she's a stout vessel, very well built, weatherly and fast. Very fast for her size. And because of her size we don't require a great number of men to manage her, which means we can carry more goods aboard. Men take up space and must be fed. As a woman of affairs yourself, you can appreciate the advantages. Our expenses are low."

"Listen to you, proud as a mother, going on about your vessel as if she was your very own child," Rachel teased. "I know nothing about ships except they are a means of escape."

It was good to feel her body soften and to hear her dove's chortle. My friend's laughter was a complex language of its own—no wonder men were charmed by her.

"Tomorrow I'll introduce you to my friend Mr. Stevenson; he can sell your cargo here. He'll get you a good price."

I shook my head. "I must sail for Havana as soon as the new rudder has been installed. Which, with any luck, will be tomorrow."

"So soon? Can't you stay awhile longer? I miss your company."

"And I yours, dear friend. But every day at anchor here costs me money I don't have. My partnership's profits depend on a quick passage with little time spent in foreign ports."

We continued along the waterfront, arm in arm. The water lapped against the pilings and the breeze brought down from the hills the scent of burning cane. All the seamen who had come ashore for the evening were now settled into the drinking establishments, the masculine roar of their voices pouring from the open doors and windows. Outside, a few low women waited silently in the shadows, looking to make a coin when the men came stumbling out.

"Do tell me, Patricia. What's it like to be a man? I've often wondered."

I smiled because she had read my thoughts. Some people, especially women, seem to have that talent. "Well, it's not easy—but it has been to my advantage."

"Is it always to your advantage?"

"Most always." Then, feeling as if I had been too smug, I said, "No. I'm being deceitful. It's difficult, pretending to be what you aren't. And very lonely at times."

We interlaced our fingers, our hands becoming one fist. My chest swelled with pent-up words—shameful feelings—seeking release. Being here with her, not having to pretend, not having to constantly prove myself, was such a happy relief! If I were truly a man I could be one of her lovers—and at that very moment I wished I were a man. A real man, not a woman pretending to be a man. I drew her to me, her slight frame easily enfolded within my arms. She rested her head against my shoulder and I realized her strength and my own vulnerability.

"It's advantageous—but is it to your liking?" Rachel pulled back and looked up at my face. "Living as a man."

I shrugged. "Mostly. I can come and go as I please."

"Don't you ever just want to be yourself?"

The breeze from the hills enveloped us like water, swirling past, carrying with it the heat and sweat of the day. "I *am* myself, Rachel. This odd creature is who I've become." I held my arms open, palms up, as if to say, *behold*.

She slipped her arms around my waist and pulled me close. "It matters not to me what guise you're in. I know you, friend. I love you."

I pressed my lips against her forehead—a kiss of friendship, not passion. I wanted both in my life—was it possible? I wanted to be both man and woman in my life—was *that* possible?

"Is there anyone in this world who knows you as I do, and loves you? Anyone beside me?"

A true friend knows the question you most want to be asked.

"There was once. I had the chance to be his wife."

"*Was* is such a sad word. Is he still alive?"

I was unable to speak for the memory, a thickness in my throat, a sting behind my eyes.

"I hope he is. But even though I dream of a reunion, I'm not entirely certain I want it. Does that make sense?"

"You may dress and talk like a man, you may captain a boat, but you think like a woman, dear friend."

"Aye." I smiled sadly, unseen in the darkness. "And that may be my downfall."

"Will you write, Patricia? Write me and tell me when you're to visit us again."

"I will," I said, burying my face in her hair, feeling her slender arms pull me close with pliant strength.

Four

Havana

"Ease sheets!"

Andromeda slowed to a drift.

"Luff up!"

George put the tiller hard over, heading the bow up into the breeze. We were nearly at a standstill.

"Let 'er go!" I called. There was a welcome splash as Moses let the anchor drop.

Before the flukes had even settled into the muddy bottom of the east side of Havana Bay, a cutter flying the Spanish flag was making its way to greet us. I was hopeful that a show of our papers and a small bribe would satisfy him, at least for a short while. If we lingered too long he'd return for more and I had little coin to spare. My plan was to make the trade quickly and leave for home as soon as possible.

First, I had to find my contact, a Habanero known to me only by the alias Sancho. Perhaps Sancho or someone in his employ had already seen us enter the harbor, or maybe the official I was about to pay off would communicate our presence to him. If not, I'd have to go ashore to find him.

We were anchored off Regla, a small fishing village in the back bay, a few miles across the water from the old city of Havana—the very same city we had besieged three years before. Our hard-won prize had been handed back to Spain in the peace treaty six months later. And the city and the fort we had taken were being rebuilt. The evidence was all around us in Havana's commodious harbor, which offered anchorage to vessels of every size and nation.

Alejandro O'Reilly, the Irish-born mercenary and advisor to the King of Spain, was overseeing the redesign and enlargement of the fort—which was to be unconquerable, or so they said. It was an ill-advised boast, in my opinion.

Meanwhile, adventurers of many nationalities were sailing here to make profits in trade. O'Reilly, that savvy ex-patriot, had essentially turned Havana into a thriving free port, at least temporarily, until the reconstruction was completed. Although, technically, Spain's trade restrictions were once again in effect, nobody seemed to pay them any mind as long as the customs officials were given their due. In fact, business was flourishing. The British, Dutch, Danes, French, and Colonials were shipping much-needed building materials and machinery, flour and other foodstuffs. We were all trying to make as much money as we could before Spain shut the door again. Havana was a goldmine for us, since coin flowed freely; for most colonists, real money was hard to come by.

My harbor fees paid, I changed into a fresh shirt and neck stock, slipped into my going-ashore waistcoat, donned wig and hat. Leaving the others on board, I made my way to a nondescript backwater pothouse on Regla's shore, where I hoped to meet my contact. This was where I had met him the last time I was here and where he had instructed me to leave word for him on my return. The landing pier was glutted with small boats three deep; I had to raft up to the outermost and step across the others to get to shore.

I stood in the doorway, perspiring, my head throbbing from the heat. I wanted to remove my stock but dared not, for fear my smooth neck might give me away.

"Aguardiente?" A woman's voice. I looked toward the bar, my eyes adjusting to the darkness inside.

"No, thank you." The cane liquor they called aguardiente was a vile spirit. A man must be low indeed to let that spirit pass his lips when he could have Rhode Island–distilled rum. "I'm here on business."

The matron laughed. "Of course you are. Everyone is here on business. But in order to do business in my establishment, you must drink." I could feel her eyes on me, sizing me up, making me uncomfortable.

"What is it?" I said peevishly. "Why do you stare?"

The mole beneath her left eye quivered ever so slightly. "You are *Inglés*."

It sounded like an accusation. My people had ravaged El Morro, destroyed their forts, diverted their water supply, and occupied their fine homes. Now that Havana was theirs again, they held us in disdain. Yet they were greedy for the goods we brought and profited as much from the trade as we did.

"I'm a colonist. A Rhode Islander."

She shrugged and allowed me a jaded smile. "I see them all, I serve them all. Havana is a regular barnyard these days. Pigs, goats, chickens, all grubbing together. But all animals must drink, no? So, what are you drinking, *Inglés*?"

"A pint of ale, señora," I said, choosing to overlook the insult. Indeed, the dirt-floored tavern sounded like a farmyard—the brays and squawks of men laughing and arguing in a variety of languages, too loud with their liquor. It smelled, too, not of hay and manure, but of men's sweat and piss.

The matron brought my ale, warm, flat, and sour. I stood at the plank of mahogany that was the bar and drank it down, and, against my better judgement, ordered a second.

"Relax, *Inglés*. Stay awhile. Nothing happens quickly in Regla.

Enjoy your supper while you wait for your agent."

It was a suggestion I couldn't refuse. If I continued drinking on an empty stomach in this heat, my head would soon be spinning. I took my second pint and found a chair by a barrel at the far end of the room beneath a small window, the louvered shutter keeping out the brilliant light and allowing a breath of air to sneak in. Here, removed from the crowd, I waited for whatever fare she was serving up. Fish, I expected, but instead it was goat stewed with peppers and plantains. I lifted the first spoonful to my mouth, found it surprisingly good. But it needed a bit of Rhode Island johnnycake to soak up the broth—and I had barrels of cornmeal in the hold to sell. Shouldn't be hard to win these cassava-eating people over to New England corn. I would have a talk with the señora; I would sell her some of Sam's good corncakes.

I kept watching the door as men came and went. Glancing around the dark room, I saw I wasn't the only one who seemed to be waiting for someone. A den of opportunists, this was, yet I was neither pirate nor thief. Newport men had a long tradition of trading in this particular fashion, yet a colonist avoiding unjust duties was quite a different animal than a common smuggler.

Quit trying to justify your actions, I counseled myself as I filled my belly with stew, drank the sour ale, and slapped at the mosquitoes humming about my ears. What did I know? Precious little when it came to laws and the rights of Englishmen. My schooling prepared me to bang at the harpsichord, make pleasantries in French, dance the quadrille, and embroider a collar—all badly. The only thing I excelled at during my schooldays was riding; I could ride a horse with the best of men. But why think of those days; they were gone and there was no one to share the memories with. Rachel, perhaps. Rachel had known me longer than anyone else alive. I missed her friendship. I might have stayed another day in Christiansted.

And where was Sancho? It had been four months since I had last seen him, but this was our designated rendezvous. Here in this squalid tavern.

My appetite was satisfied, and my thirst quenched, having finished the goat and peppers and plantains and two pints of ale. I was making my way through a carafe of cheap Spanish wine when I felt a presence. From across the room a man was looking at me. I returned his gaze. Sancho? No. My cheeks flushed but I kept my eyes on his, not so much to invite as to challenge. A moment later he picked up his glass and walked toward me, easily navigating the crowded room. Was this an intermediary Sancho had sent in his place? He looked quite appealing in his bleached white shirt, open at the neck to reveal his Adam's apple and the hollow beneath it. His well-cut breeches and flawless stockings gave him the air of having just stepped out of the haberdasher's shop. Much better dressed than Sancho.

The next instant I recognized him. My head reeled and my tongue went numb. How does a man greet a former enemy and captor? Frantically I gathered my wits.

"Lieutenant Guyon, what a surprise seeing you here," I said as coolly as I could manage, rising to my feet. He was taller than I remembered and even more attractive.

The Frenchman's bow was deep enough to be respectful. "*Tout le plaisir est pour moi*, Dr. MacPherson. Indeed, it is my pleasure."

My heart was knocking ridiculously in my chest, and I'm certain my face was a beacon. "You have keen eyes, sir, to recognize me across the room. In fact, to remember me at all."

He regarded me with a frank appreciation that was startling— it was like we had once been lovers instead of enemies. "I never forget a ship, or a face. I watched you sail into the bay this afternoon and recognized your vessel at once. Such a prize *Andromeda* was." His face, so beautifully composed. An enigmatic smile played on his lips and lit up his dark eyes. "We never finished that game of backgammon we began in my cabin."

What now to say to the man who once took *Andromeda* and held me captive? I had bargained for our release and won it; Guyon had been a gentleman and honored the terms. But the war was over and everyone was working to rebuild Havana. Yes, there had been a mutual attraction, then as now. I couldn't deny it—but I was determined not to play his game. Instead, I changed the subject.

"How is your captain's health? Captain Renwez?"

Guyon gave me a Frenchman's dismissive shrug, annoying me. My head was a battleground of conflicting emotions.

"I hardly know. I've not seen Renwez since the war's end. I'm told he has retired to a little cottage back in Bretagne. Raising cabbages, they say. With one less tooth to give him pain, thanks to you." He caught my eyes again and held them. "I am my own captain now."

"Well then. Captain Guyon. Congratulations on your advancement." My voice sounded on the edge, breathless, rising out of control. I fought to rein it in.

His eyes danced; he clearly enjoyed my discomfort and allowed me to stumble on.

"Or perhaps, now that the war's over, you have retired? A gentleman of leisure now?"

"*Au contraire;* I'm quite engaged at the moment. *Muy ocupado,* as the Habaneros say."

"You're working for Spain, I presume?"

"I work for my own gain. As do you, MacPherson, I would venture to guess." His dark eyes teased; he clearly knew he had the advantage. And I knew I was in over my head in this repartee.

"I would ask you to join me, Guyon, but there seems to be a shortage of chairs. Don't let me interrupt your supper. It was a pleasure to see you again."

He completely ignored my dismissal. "Such an unfortunate little pothouse, so ill-appointed. Not known for its food or its clientele. Tell me, MacPherson, have you seen the city of Havana by night?"

Memories of the siege came, unbidden. The horrors of the bush camp up on the ridge where Dudley Freeman and I tried to save lives. Where more men fell sick from tropical fever than died by cannon, musket, or sword. Where I fell sick and might have died in the destruction of El Morro, had not Brian Dalton come to my aid.

I smiled blandly. "No. I've never taken the opportunity. I'm not here for pleasure."

"A pity. Havana is such an alluring city. But I have a chair for you at my humble table. Will you do me the honor of joining me?"

"I'm sorry, I don't intend to stay long. Actually, I'm here on business matters. Trade."

He smiled as if holding in a great mirth. "Yes, of course you are, as am I. We're all here on business matters. We're all here to trade. But please, allow me the pleasure of your company while you wait. At my expense."

How could I refuse? I didn't want to refuse. Damn him!

"One drink with you, sir. I can't stay long. I've only just arrived, and I have a ship to attend to."

I followed him across the room, weaving in and out between the tables of traders and fishermen, following him to his table. He pulled out a rough-hewn chair for me with a flourish, as if I were a lady. And when we were seated, he poured me a glass from his bottle. There were, I noticed, two glasses, as if he had been expecting someone.

"Shall we play cards or roll the dice for amusement while you wait for your contact?"

"I've told you, I'm not a gaming man." Again, the smile, his eyes filled with the knowledge of my secret.

"I believe you are quite adept at games. *Le jeu c'est tout, n'est-ce pas?*" He lifted his glass, waiting for me to lift mine. "Once enemies, now friends."

"Friends? On what basis?" I challenged weakly, my insides beginning to go soft as butter in the sun. The Frenchman had a way of manipulating my emotions, of directing my response the way a skillful dancer leads his partner.

"Fate has flung us together again. Come, let us be friends," he urged. "Give me a chance to make amends."

"I bear you no will, Guyon."

"*Eh bien*, that's a start." He smiled warmly in victory, extending his glass. "To our détente—the first step in friendship."

"Do you always have an extra glass?"

"Of course. It's not good to drink alone and one never knows who one will meet in a tavern, *n'est-ce pas*? All of the best deals are made over wine."

Touching his glass to mine caused me to catch my breath. The wine filled my mouth with its velvet complexity. It was a lovely vintage—far better than the house rot I had ordered.

"There, that's better. Now, let me guess, is it the man called Sancho you're waiting for? Ah yes, I thought so," he tsk-tsked. "Sancho is unreliable. It's unfortunate you have fallen in with him. My friend Renaldo is much more trustworthy. Shall we drink to our fortunes?"

"Our fortunes?" I laughed at the exaggeration. To think a shorthanded merchant schooner could make a fortune was ludicrous. But the Frenchman did not laugh. He seemed quite serious.

"Money brings us all to Havana, does it not? The richest city in the hemisphere, the best harbor. Why the British returned it to the Spanish is quite beyond me. Ah, but they kept the cold Canadian provinces, didn't they? That wouldn't have been my choice."

"Nor mine. But no one asked me."

Now it was his turn to laugh. "We can't direct the course of history; we can only look out for ourselves." Then, leaning across the table as if to confide in me, he said, "Shall we continue our discussion elsewhere? I would love to show you the city of Havana at night."

My heart bumped with an eagerness I found disconcerting. "I told you, lieutenant, I have business to attend to. I'm waiting to close my deal."

"Captain," he corrected, with a smile.

"Right. *Captain* Guyon. And I am now *Captain* MacPherson."

"Captain MacPherson," Guyon said, validating me. I noticed his thick dark hair was streaked with gray. "So you've given up the surgical trade?"

"I can still pull a tooth. Or dig out a bullet. Or remove a gangrenous limb, should the occasion arise."

"I have no doubt of that." His eyes never left mine. "We have a lot in common, you and I."

"You're French and I'm English, remember?"

Again the smile, the seductive smile. "A man can't help where he was born. Remember our détente."

I ran my finger around the rim of the glass, buying time to think. Yet I could think of nothing, my mind was awhirl. "What is it you want from me, Guyon?"

"Information."

"Information?" I smiled. "I'm sorry to disappoint you, but I'm simply a trader. I'm carrying cornmeal, candles, cobblestones, and rum. Information, I have none."

"You have more information than you realize. Tell me, Captain MacPherson, what do the men of Newport say of the new tax your Parliament has imposed? Are they playing by the rules or do they ignore it? Who supports it and who does not?"

"What does it matter to you? Much of what I hear is gossip."

"Gossip, too, is a form of intelligence; some of it is quite valuable."

"Valuable? To whom?"

"To the men who are rebuilding Havana."

"The Spaniards? Even if I had information, why should I sell it to the Spaniards?"

"Why not? Someone is going to profit; it might as well be you and me. But it's not just the Spaniards who are in the market for information. The Habaneros, the Creoles of this remarkable old city, are eager for it as well. They have their own agenda, apart from their mother country. And the French—they're the greatest purveyors of intrigue, I assure you."

He leaned over the table toward me, to be heard without shouting over the dull roar of conversation and laughter. "Intelligence is the perfect cargo. It doesn't spoil, it doesn't take space in the hold, there's no duty to pay."

Guyon picked up his wine glass and swirled it, staring at it intently, allowing me time to reflect on the possibility. It was all rather vague and mysterious. I didn't know what exactly was expected of me, nor did I know the risks involved. But I was intrigued, I had to admit.

"What exactly are you proposing?"

"I'd like to introduce you to some of my associates. The men who buy what we have to sell. You can decide for yourself if you wish to do business with them. We have much in common, you and I. Fortune has brought us together again and she is smiling. It would be a good alliance."

How would we work together, I wondered? What would be expected of me? Were there any guarantees? What were the risks? I didn't want to appear naïve or too eager.

"I'd like to meet these men, your associates. But my primary purpose here is to complete my transaction. I have partners and investors to answer to."

Guyon drained his glass, savoring the last mouthful. "But why waste the time spent waiting?"

I didn't answer, instead looked to the door. Two more men had just entered.

"That is not your man, but he will be here shortly; I'll leave you to your rendezvous. But you may find Sancho's terms less favorable than you would like. The rules of the game here have changed, you'll find. Perhaps I can be of some assistance. If you care to find me, my vessel is the *Osprey*. A Bermuda sloop."

"A Bermuda sloop?" I couldn't hide my envy. These Bermuda-built vessels were known for their raked masts and their stiff hulls, which gave them great maneuverability. Designed by a Dutchman, they say, in the last century, and now built by Bermudian slaves of Bermudian cedar. Like our man Moses, the Blacks were excellent shipwrights and joiners, and their sloops were in great demand.

Guyon couldn't contain his pride. "She's a beauty, prettier than a French corvette. She'd be a grand privateer but the last war is over and the next one hasn't yet begun; but there is always something to transport, *n'est-ce pas*?"

Duty-free goods, of course.

"I hope we can be friends, you and I." He met my eyes again, his expression becoming serious. Slowly he pushed back his chair and rose to his feet.

I stood up too, wondering whether to offer him my hand in the cordial Colonial fashion or to remain aloof. Guyon bowed slightly, with the ease of a courtier, and touched the corner of his hat. Then reaching into his pocket, he placed a coin on the table to pay our account and walked out into the night. Leaving me in a tangle of suspicion and desire.

Sancho showed up soon after. I invited him to sit down at my table, where we closed our deal over the rest of Guyon's bottle. Sancho wanted everything we had aboard, offering in exchange sixty-three hogsheads of molasses, two dozen cowhides, and a pipe of Madeira wine. I asked for seventy-six hogsheads of molasses, he countered with sixty-nine, and we agreed on seventy-four. I mistakenly felt quite pleased with myself.

"I'll send a lighter and four men to your vessel first thing in the morning. We'll unload your cargo and I'll give you the pipe of Madeira. As soon as I have the molasses, I'll deliver it to you, along with the hides."

"How soon?"

"Maybe a week." He shrugged. "Maybe longer."

"I can't afford to be idle, sitting at anchor. What guarantee do I have?"

"My reputation is my guarantee. We've done business before; you know I'm dependable. Besides, my friend, there are many pleasures in Havana for you to take advantage of while you're waiting for the goods. Perhaps you'd like a woman? A young girl? Pure white, black as night, or any shade in between. We have them all, sweet as molasses, available for a song."

"I have no need of a female, just the goods, Sancho."

He clicked his tongue in mockery. "You *Inglés* are so impatient, yet your blood runs cool. What hot-blooded male would turn down such an opportunity?"

"Perhaps we should call the deal off," I chanced. "There are many other agents eager for my cargo."

The Habanero smiled, showing his stained teeth. "A bird in the hand is worth two in the bush, isn't that what your people say? Molasses takes time. The roads from the plantations are bad from the recent rains. We can hardly keep up with the demand."

"Money, then. Reals."

"Silver also takes time to obtain."

I recognized the game. The longer he kept me waiting, the more anxious I'd be to settle. "How much time?"

He picked at his teeth with a dirty fingernail. "Things are very busy here, but you're a good man to do business with. I will try to expedite matters. Do you suppose you can get for me two pairs of your Narragansett pacers, next run? I can get you a good price for them."

I gave Cyrus the night off. He took the ship's boat across the bay to Havana proper, which offered more prospects and excitement than sleepy little Regla, while I remained aboard, on deck, enjoying the night air and my wine-softened head. From the new fort a cannon boomed ceremoniously, announcing the closing of the harbor for the night, and the great chain guarding the entrance was winched up off the harbor floor.

A bumping alongside, a soft *ahoy*. My heart leapt like a dolphin as I dropped him a line, but I was determined not to show it. A moment later Guyon scrambled up over the bulwark and onto *Andromeda*'s deck.

"I've spoken with the harbormaster; he's a friend of mine. He'll ignore you for at least a week."

"And what do I owe you for your interference? I fear it is more than I can afford."

"You don't owe me anything. It was simply a gesture of my

goodwill."

"I suppose I should thank you." I searched his face in the darkness, seeing an earnest smile.

"Though, I admit, I hope to buy time. Time for you to entertain my proposition."

"And what exactly is your proposition?"

"*Un accord d'affaires.* A business alliance. Friendship. Whatever you choose. We would make a good pair, you and I."

"Out of the question." This was a dangerous yet alluring flirtation I was participating in.

He stepped closer, close enough to kiss me, and I wanted it. That, and more. I wanted it very much.

"You're mad, Guyon."

"You're quite right, I am mad, you make me so," he said quietly, so as not to be heard by the others aboard, asleep belowdecks, or so I hoped.

"That's absurd," I demurred. "Most unnatural."

"There's nothing unnatural about it," he said in a low, matter-of-fact voice. "I knew you for a woman the first time we met."

I had felt certain he had seen through my disguise, though he had never said so directly. He never challenged me, never before called my bluff. All hints and innuendoes. Now it was out in plain view, like a chemise on the clothesline.

"What was it that gave me away?" I whispered. "My voice? How did you know?"

His pupils widened and he leaned closer, removing my tricorn, our noses nearly touching. "Had I been blind and deaf I would have known."

I took the offensive, found his mouth, wanting to kiss not to be kissed—but I wasn't prepared for my own response, a giving way, a surrender. Suddenly I stepped back, snatching my hat from his hands, breathless.

"You must go, Guyon," I said. "It's late."

"Not too late, I hope. Remember our game of backgammon—we never finished it."

"I told you. I detest games."

I felt his smile in the darkness. "My dear, life itself is a game, a grand game. Best to have a good partner. Someone who knows your mind and can back your play."

The Frenchman was one of the very few who had seen through my disguise at once. It was as if he had stripped me to bare flesh with his eyes. Yet he had not tried to take advantage of me during those hours I was his captive, nor had he exposed me. He was self-serving, yes, that I knew. Still, the desire was there, an enormous and powerful presence I couldn't deny.

Guyon lifted his hat. "I respect your wishes, captain. No games. But do allow me to enjoy the pleasure of your company while we are here in Havana. Surely, that can have no adverse consequences."

With that he disappeared over the gunwale and cast off, leaving me alone with my conflicting desires.

Five

Havana

The day dawned rosy and warm. True to his word, Sancho arrived with his lighter at sunrise. He inspected our cornmeal and rum, tasting a little more of the rum than was necessary to deem it satisfactory.

After the barrels had been off-loaded and taken to the fishing shed that served as a temporary warehouse, Sancho's men returned for the cobblestones, brought up from the hold in buckets and hoisted over the side onto the lighter's broad deck, and then towed to the fort at the mouth of the bay. Now our hold was empty, ready to take on our molasses and hides as soon as they arrived. I didn't like being at a disadvantage; I wanted to get in and out of this port as quickly as possible. Who knew when Spain's hammer would come down and we'd all be run out of the harbor? Just like that, a profitable run could become a total loss. In the meantime, the men had to be fed. And paid. Moses and Sam, hired out by Dominic, had an arrangement to keep fifty percent of their wages on the books; they were saving to buy their freedom, which Dominic had promised them. Raised a Quaker, he had an aversion to slavery, though not so much, apparently, that he emancipated them immediately. My partner was too tight-fisted for that.

After the cargo was unloaded, we set about preparing *Andromeda* for the return passage. I paced the deck impatiently, noticing everything that needed attention—the iron rings and fittings that wanted blacking and oiling, the chafed lines, the sails that needed airing and a patch or two. The ship's bottom was already growing a beard in these waters; the clinging barnacles and seaweed would slow our passage home. I set George, Moses, and Sam to work on the foredeck, patching sails, and Cyrus back by the mainmast to short-splice the throat halyard where it had chafed during the passage. He was unusually quiet, working with a forced concentration, his tar-stained fingers teasing the fibers of hemp with the fid's point.

"I trust you had a gay time of it ashore?"

He gave me a wry smile. "The local spirit they drink here? I definitely do not recommend it."

"Aguardiente? I could have told you that," I said. "Stick to small beer. It's sour and will bloat your belly but it won't wreck your head or steal your soul like aguardiente."

"Another cup of coffee might help," he cajoled.

"Coffee is the only known antidote. Unfortunately, there are only the bitter grounds left in the pot. But tell me, did you enjoy your time ashore?"

"I did. The ladies here are so accommodating." His face brightened. "I can't wait to go back. Besides, I have some unfinished business with a certain scoundrel at a certain pothouse."

"Don't be a hothead, Cyrus; we can't afford any trouble. I need you to set an example. Oh, and when you're finished splicing the halyard will you please organize the men to obtain water for our return trip? I want to sail as soon as we're loaded. You'll find good water at the aqueduct for just a few pesos." I handed him a leather purse of coins. "The men have their own adventures they'll want to trade, I'm sure. Set a fine example for them and keep everyone out of mischief."

He flashed me an innocent smile.

"Later this evening I'm going ashore; I'll be quite late," I said.

He raised an eyebrow quizzically.

"On business," I felt compelled to add. "I'm meeting someone who could prove to be a valuable connection for us in the future. I need you back on board by dark, do you understand?"

He nodded. "We'll be back with the water by dark."

The men ashore, I had the ship to myself for a few hours. There was much to be done but I found it hard to concentrate. Instead I stared for long minutes at two pelicans diving for fish. Such ungainly creatures, yet, apparently, they were successful. I felt an affinity for them, a strange kinship. I watched the birds fishing for their supper but more than once my eyes wandered across the bay, looking for his Bermudian sloop. Finding it. Looking away.

The wind came up. It started to rain. A cloudburst, violent and short-lived as only those in warm climes can be. I took shelter under the canvas awning, glad for the rain washing my deck of salt from the passage, and glad to see the anchor was holding well as the wind tugged at us. Half an hour later it was all over; the squall had passed, leaving the air fresh and the sky a benevolent blue. Later, the men returned with enough freshwater for our passage home.

That night Guyon showed me Havana. Even though I had been among the besiegers I had never set foot inside the great old city proper. Besides the anchorage, all I had known of the great Havana were the mosquito-infested jungles up on the heights where Dudley Freeman and I had been sent to operate a field hospital during the invasion.

There was an ancient feel to the city, the mineral smell of coquina walls embedded with shells from the seabed, a restless stirring of the languid air, as if the ghosts of the dispossessed Indians drifted down from the hills every night to take back what had once been theirs. What was the allure of this place? It's very location on the earth, I supposed. A waypoint for treasure ships from the fabled Spanish Main, and an entrepôt for adventurers, pirates, freebooters, and prostitutes from all over the world.

We pushed our way through the squares, alive with people, people of every race.

Music floated above us and through us, a medley of strumming from taverns, courtyards, and squares as we elbowed our way through a river of people

"I want to show you El Arsenal," Guyon said, leading the way back to the water, to the royal shipyard where at least a dozen vessels were under construction. Workers camped in the dark shadows of the hulls and guards patrolled the yard. The smell of fresh sawdust hung on the evening air.

"Look there." Guyon pointed to a massive frame on blocks in the center of the shipyard. "That one is designed by Mullan. He knows the Spanish taste for ostentation."

"Mullan? Should I know him?"

"Mateo Mullan. He's another dispossessed Irishman in the service of Spain. Using Spain against Britain. The enemy of my enemy, as they say."

Our bombs during the siege had not reached the shipyard—one of the finest in the New World. Clearly, Havana intended to reclaim her wealth and status.

From El Arsenal we walked to the new plaza where the new cathedral was being constructed—it would rival any in Europe, and, like those in Europe, it would take many more years to be completed. The paving of the square had begun, and could see firsthand where my shipment of cobblestones might be used. We supped at a tavern just off the Plaza de Armas, still packed with officers and tradesmen eating, drinking, and gaming. The beer here was good, brewed from New England barley, Guyon told me, and much superior to the beer at Sancho's pothouse on Regla's shore.

"Will you accompany me to a private gathering tomorrow night? There are some men I'd like you to meet. Friends of the lieutenant governor."

"Really, Guyon, I think you've confused me with someone important. Not to mention, I'd rather your friends didn't know I was here. They may not take kindly to me. With any luck I'll hear from Sancho tomorrow. With any luck I'll be gone in a few days."

"You're missing the point." He leaned forward across the tabletop. "Never mind Sancho and his petty dealings. What I have in mind for you—for us—is much bigger. Can't you see? I'm well-connected with the men who operate the new Havana. I've made connections in New Orleans and Santa Cruz. We can do well for ourselves here; we can make our own little fortune."

Why did he want to include me? What could I possibly offer? If he wanted a woman, he could easily get one. Surely there were any number of wealthy Creoles with beautiful, well-endowed daughters, plenty of lively widows with fortunes looking for a handsome man with a ship.

"You do not say no, so I will take that as a yes." He reached for his glass. "*Eh bien,* it's settled. I'll come for you at sunset."

Six

Havana

The next day passed. I heard nothing from Sancho. *Andromeda* was provisioned and ready to sail on the tide—as soon as our trade goods were on board.

Guyon came for me at sunset, as promised, rowing his own boat. We walked along the newly cobbled Calle Mercaderes toward the host's *palacio* near the Plaza de Armas, making our way through a throng of people. It was a holiday, some saint's day or festival, and all around us a buoyant atmosphere of merrymaking, shrieks of laughter, the babble of voices, scraps of sentences in various languages. There is no place better for a private conversation than a crowded street, especially one in a foreign city. He briefed me on some of the men I would meet tonight, particularly our host, Juan de Miralles, a successful merchant with many connections and somewhat obscure beginnings. Miralles had been born in the Alicante region of Spain, to French parents who curried some sort of favor with the Spanish king. He came to Havana as a young man and married into a well-to-do family.

"I feel at a great disadvantage," I admitted. "My Spanish is poor; I only know a few phrases."

"Don't fret. Miralles is multilingual; he'll speak to you in English."

"You speak Spanish, do you not?"

"I do." He cocked an eyebrow. "Though often it's an advantage to pretend not to. An asset, I assure you, when buying and selling intelligence."

I felt at a disadvantage and disliked being condescended to, but there was nothing to be done about it. Would I be scorned for being English? Would I be reviled for having taken part in the siege that knocked down their fort and brought their city to its knees? Or had it? A new fort was being built in its place, far bigger than the Morro Castle our sappers and gunners had destroyed.

"Don't worry," Guyon assured me with a wave of his hand. "The British victory was good for Habaneros, if not so good for the motherland. Everyone in Havana is profiting, but the good times won't last forever. The trick is to recognize opportunities and grab them. That's what Miralles is particularly adept at. And no one holds *you* personally responsible."

Still, I felt ill at ease. My wig was looking a bit shabby; it needed to be dressed. My coat wanted brushing, and my shoes—my shoes were hopelessly worn down in the heels and saltwater-stained. Guyon said my wardrobe was of little importance.

"No one will give it a second thought. English colonists aren't known for their sense of style, MacPherson, my dear. And standing next to a Spaniard, even a Frenchman looks dowdy. Have no fear, you fit the part perfectly."

"Oh, so now you insult me? Really, Guyon, what is it you want of me?"

"Your presence. It excites me," he said playfully.

"So, this is all sport? I'm playing a part to please your imagination?"

I was so blunt, having no practice in the art of flirtation. I was not a beautiful woman, I knew it. I didn't think of myself as pretty, comely, or fair. My skin was covered with a mass of freckles, my hands rough, my temper sharp. Beneath my peruke my scalp was a washerwoman's scrub brush, yet Guyon said he admired my cheekbones. My ears. The curvaceous line of my upper lip. He was entranced, he said, by my temperament. No one had ever admired that, which is why I could not allow myself to believe him.

"Don't toy with me, Guyon."

"But you are attractive, and the fact you don't know it makes you all the more desirable. In truth, I believe you have information my friends will find useful. Certainly your ability to disguise your sex can be of use. You can profit from this association, I assure you."

"I believe you've mistaken me for a spy."

"You could be a spy—and a good one, I should think. Rather like the artful Chevalier d'Eon." He laughed and slid his arm around my shoulders in a brotherly fashion as we walked along the dark street. I liked the weight of his forearm, the grip of his hand on my upper arm. When at last he withdrew it I felt much too light, as if I would float away like wood smoke.

"Monsieur d'Eon," I said. "The French diplomat. He served as dragoon captain in the war, did he not? I've heard it said that d'Eon is really a woman."

"That's the rumor. One of the rumors. Then again, d'Eon may be a man pretending to be a woman pretending to be a man. In any case, le Chevalier d'Eon has served France well."

"But I am a simple trader, trying to make a living."

"So you would have us believe."

"What is it you think I know, Guyon?"

"You know the collective mind of the men of Newport. No doubt you drink coffee with Rhode Island's malcontents. No doubt you know these so-called Sons of Liberty? Are they connected to Boston's faction?"

I shook my head. "Actually, I keep a rather low profile. My present income does not afford me much time in the coffeehouses and taverns."

"All that can change tonight. Your means are about to improve."

I felt a warm glow of possibility, of opportunity.

"You and I would be fantastic as partners. I do hope you'll consider it, MacPherson." He gave me a teasing smile. "May I call you Patrick?"

The devil—he was enjoying this game. "If you must know, my name is Patricia."

"Then may I call you Patricia? Only when we're alone, of course."

Hearing a man speak my given name softened me. It had been a long time. "Don't assume we're going to be alone often."

"Now you dash my hopes again."

"You know my first name; it's only fair you tell me yours."

"I thought you'd never ask. Olivier Jean Paul."

"Olivier Jean Paul Guyon." I tried it out using my best French accent, which was not so good. "You have an abundance of names, sir."

"*Oui*," he laughed. "*C'est vrai.* Perhaps my only inheritance. My father wanted to honor his grandfather Jean Paul, but my mother insisted upon Olivier, who I suspect may have been a former lover. You may call me whatever you like, I shall answer to it."

"Then I shall continue to call you Guyon."

A drunkard stumbled out of a dark passage, lurching toward us. He might have knocked me down except Guyon instinctively pulled me close against him, out of harm's way. The man only brushed against us, and ricocheted off harmlessly, staggering on, oblivious. But Guyon held me a moment longer than was necessary. It had been so long since I had been pressed against a man's person like that, I had forgotten their blind, urgent need. Feeling it, my blood went hot. My head filled with his particular smell and I wanted to follow my desire but instead pulled away, struggling to regain my balance, my separate space, my identity.

"Stop, please. I am completely out of my element here." I straightened my hat and tugged self-consciously at the cravat tied around my throat.

"How I would love to remove that cravat for you."

"Enough!"

"As you wish. I won't speak of it again, but you can't stop me from wanting to."

Men are designed so simply, I thought. That was part of their strength. They knew what they wanted, what they needed, and from whom. From us it was that one favor. A smart woman uses that need to her advantage to get what she wants in return. But I had never been practiced in the art of manipulation. Like a man, I wanted direct power, not indirect influence. And what did I want from Guyon? I wanted what he wanted, I recognized that. I wanted to satisfy that hunger, quench that thirst. But doing so could be dangerous to my way of life, as it had been once before. With him. Aboard the frigate. It had led to my dismissal, the end of my career as a surgeon's mate.

Seven

Palacio de Miralles

"Allow me to introduce my good friend Patrick MacPherson—trader, shipmaster, and former naval surgeon from the colony of Rhode Island."

"Pleased to make your acquaintance." I doffed my hat and nodded.

Miralles flashed a courtly smile but I felt his deep-set eyes on me, taking my measure, sizing me up.

"*Bienvenido*, gentlemen. Please, follow me to the *saleta*."

Hidden behind thick coral walls, the host's *palacio* was a private world inside the city. Through the inner courtyard and up the stairs to the spacious salon where a group of men—Spaniards, Habaneros, expatriate Irish and French—stood conversing over drinks. I soon had a glass of wine in my hand and was engaged in a conversation that transitioned smoothly to English on my arrival. I realized at once that these men were well read, well informed, and most interested in what I had to say. Though of different backgrounds, we were bound together by common interests; our futures and fortunes were dependent on free trade among the colonies.

Amid talk of the rebuilding of the fort and the activity at the shipyard were oblique references to goods shipped in and out of Havana. The city had been opened up like an oyster and there was no going back. Spain had relaxed her restrictive trade policies and now taxed everyone. Miralles was seemingly profiting from the open-port policy. From what Guyon had told me, our host traded with merchants in Saint Augustine, Charlestown, and Philadelphia, as well as the West Indian ports.

Had Guyon told Miralles, or any of them, my secret? If he had, they showed no signs of knowing. They spoke freely and roughly, as men speak when in their own company. Perhaps my former enemy was to be trusted. The fine red wine in my goblet began to expand my mind to the possibilities that an association with Guyon might offer and how I could profit by it.

I turned to him and commented on the painted wood ceiling overhead. "A Moorish design?"

"Moorish, yes. *Mudejar*, as they say here. Did you notice the exquisite tile work in the entrance hall? At least the British bombs didn't reach this far, eh, MacPherson?" He gave me a jesting smile and touched his goblet against mine. "To Havana's reconstruction—may we both prosper from it."

Somewhere inside the great house a clock struck ten, echoed by the bells from the nearby cathedral. Conversations paused until the last bell had ceased to ring.

"Very sweet-sounding bells, are they not?" Juan de Miralles said, leading me toward the open window. "There is the cathedral; you can see the bell tower. La Catedral de la Vergen Maria de la Concepcion Immaculada de La Habana." The church's Spanish name rolled musically off his tongue.

Looking out, I saw the dark shape rising over the rooftops. Not yet completed, the stone building would be the largest in this part of the world—this hemisphere.

"Do you know why her bells ring more sweetly than most, captain?"

I waited for his answer, realizing I had been set up for it.

"Precious metals were mixed with the bronze when the bells were cast. The sweet sound you hear is that of silver and gold. Imagine—Spain has so much of it she melts it down and casts it into bells."

"Remarkable," I said. "Though I can think of more practical uses for it."

Miralles laughed. "Quite right, sir, and spoken like a Yankee. Armament, for example. Think of all the weapons such wealth could purchase. Gunpowder and shot make quite a sound too, and just as sweet to some."

"I'm quite sure there's money to be made in guns, but for the moment I'm enjoying the peace—and the opportunity to buy molasses from you."

"Peace is sweet, but too much is cloying. Your people are a feisty lot, I understand. Is it true the Newport mob fired on a British naval vessel?"

"The *Saint John* incident?"

"Were you there? Did you see it?"

"I was in Newport when it happened, yes."

"What triggered the incident?"

"An unlawful seizure by Lieutenant Hill, in command of His Majesty's schooner *Saint John*. The lieutenant seized a vessel he suspected of smuggling. And he went ashore to press Newport watermen."

"What happened?"

"There was a fight. The King's schooner fired a shot to recall her crew but not before our boys pelted them with stones from the wharf and our gunners at the fort fired shots over *Saint John*'s bow."

"A bold and admirable show of resistance," Miralles said. "From what I hear, Rhode Islanders are ungovernable."

"Not ungovernable, sir. Self-governable."

"And what of the *Maidstone* affair?"

"When *Maidstone* came to Newport to press our watermen, a group seized the ship's longboat from the dock and dragged it to the Newport Commons, where they set it on fire."

"Were they backed by the Committee? As in Boston?"

"Backed—or perhaps fronted by them. Though it doesn't take much to incite such acts. There's much contention and fighting amongst Rhode Islanders, but on some matters we all unite."

"That's what we're counting on, MacPherson. British colonists uniting." His dark eyes sparked, brimming with ideas. "Should your Committee, your Sons of Liberty as they are called, need muskets, I have a ready source. Powder and ball as well."

"Liberty's Daughters are waging a war without arms," I said.

Miralles cocked an eyebrow. "Liberty's Daughters?"

"The good women of New England have taken up the loom and are wearing homespun again, instead of buying cloth imported from Britain. They've developed a taste for coffee instead of John Company's tea. Women of every means are tightening the household purse strings to squeeze the English merchants. Since we have no direct voice in Parliament, our cousins must convince them."

"Very brave of the ladies to sacrifice their frippery. Still, it never hurts to have a well-stocked arsenal at the ready."

I nodded, smiling, but had no interest in buying arms.

A servant appeared, interrupting with an apology and a bow, and handed Miralles an envelope. I politely looked away, gazing out the window, pretending to look at the cathedral, though I could see him, peripherally. He read the message in a matter of seconds, dismissed the servant with a nod and refolded the paper, slipping it inside his waistcoat like an afterthought. "May I have a word with you in private, captain?" His expression revealed nothing, though his face had flushed and his focus seemed to be elsewhere.

I followed Miralles onto the balcony overlooking the inner courtyard, catching a fleeting scent of jasmine on the warm air. A chorus of insects sang, unseen, adding a rich, dense layer of sound to the night. The host pulled two cigars from his pocket and offered me one. Snipped off the end of his cigar and handed me the silver cutter so that I could do the same. He then took a reed from the spill box on the colonnade, lit it in the sconce's flame and toasted the foot of his cigar. Puffing vigorously, he passed the burning reed to me. I didn't care to smoke and seldom indulged, but living among men had taught me the ritual. The first inhalation of the sweet sot weed went straight to my head.

Now Miralles got to the point. "Monsieur Guyon says you are quite handy with a knife. He sings your praises as a surgeon. He tells me you once saved his captain's life. During the war. When you were detained by his ship."

I suppressed a cough, pretended to clear my throat. "Monsieur Guyon exaggerates, sir. I am trained as a surgeon, yes. I served as surgeon's mate during the war. I'm a good surgeon, yes. But I wouldn't go so far as to say I saved his captain's life, though I did do him a service."

"Then you're no longer practicing your arts?"

"Trade is more profitable," I hedged. "But I keep my instruments sharp, just in case."

Miralles nodded. "Always on the ready. That's good, very good. Perhaps you could be of assistance to one of our friends. A very important man here in Havana."

I took a leisurely draw on my cigar, thinking of what to say. "If I can be of service, I am willing, certainly. But surely there are well-qualified surgeons and physicians here in Havana?"

"Yes, of course," he said, a bit impatiently. "We have an abundance of surgeons, apothecaries, medical doctors." He dropped his voice. "But this is a very private matter of which I speak. A matter concerning a certain nobleman's daughter. It's a delicate situation, you see. He does not want the whole city to know about the young doña's condition. It would ruin her chances of making the best possible match."

Surely, he did not expect me to terminate a pregnancy? "I see. I'm afraid I must decline, sir."

Miralles looked out over the leafy spread of tree boughs in the courtyard garden. "She has been brought to childbed. She labors."

"May God be with her," I said, relieved. Childbirth was managed well enough by midwives.

"Ah, that's the problem, MacPherson. God is with her. Or she is with God—in the Santa Clara convent where she has been placed until a good match could be made for her. Nonetheless, she has managed to compromise herself, even inside the cloister, though the Clares are known for scoffing at the laws of enclosure."

"How old is she?"

"Nearly fifteen. Her father had an elegant coming-of-age ceremony planned for her, but that has been postponed."

I felt a stab of sympathy for her. Was she a rebellious girl? Impetuous and in love? Or had someone in a position of power taken advantage of her?

"She is very young for childbirth, and first deliveries are notoriously long," I said. "Surely there are midwives to attend her?"

"Midwives? Of course, there are midwives, but this is a delicate matter, as I've said. The family's social reputation is at stake. She is to be wed to a *peninsular*, a blue-blood who expects her to be pure as part of the bargain. The sisters of the convent are caring for her in childbed and they are trusted to keep secrets, but I have sources who tell me things aren't progressing as they should. She grows weak, yet the child is still not delivered. The doña's father, our friend, is beside himself with worry. And he's a very religious man."

White ash fell slowly from the end of his cigar onto the tiled floor. He paid it no mind.

I blew a slow stream of smoke out over the balcony rail. "Yes. But why me?"

"It cannot be a man of Havana." He turned to face me directly, his face beseeching. "Our friend would be grateful if a man of medicine, one unknown in these parts, would intervene and do whatever is necessary to save his daughter's life, while protecting her privacy and maintaining her reputation."

"And the infant?"

"And saving the infant too, if possible. While he can't acknowledge the baby as his own grandchild, if it looks to be of pure blood our friend could raise it as he would raise a natural son or daughter, one of his own born out of wedlock."

I felt a pang of self-pity, for I knew all too well how gentlemen raised their bastard children.

"But if the blood is tainted..." Miralles studied the glowing cigar, rolling it between his well-manicured fingers.

"Tainted?"

"If his daughter delivers an infant of mixed blood it will soon become apparent. If that's the case, the child will be brought up in the convent, raised to be a servant for the Clares. In any case, the secret stays in the convent. The sisters can be trusted, but knowledge of the birth must not escape those walls, or the doña's value as a match will be destroyed. She is her father's only living legitimate offspring. If there's anything you can do..."

"I'm no accoucheur, sir," I protested. "If your friend's daughter needed bleeding or cupping, I'd be happy to oblige. If she needed a tooth pulled or a boil lanced, or a gangrenous leg removed—those are my forte. Those are the interventions I'm skilled at."

"Not my friend's daughter—*our* friend's daughter," Miralles corrected. "I cannot yet tell you who he is, though I assure you he is a friend to you. I cannot tell you his name though you'll discover it in time." He looked at me with such earnestness I felt myself swept into deep waters. I knew not what to say. Childbirth was a most unpredictable affair, more a force of nature than an illness to be cured.

"I realize you're not a midwife; I don't wish to insult you. Instead, I am imploring you. A discreet intervention by an unknown surgeon with such an excellent reputation as Guyon assures me you have— that would make our friend appreciative. It would make him very grateful toward you. And me. And it would do much to repair the bad reputation the British have earned during the recent occupation."

He looked up at the patch of night sky now illuminated by a

swelling moon and seemed to study it, giving me time to overcome my reluctance.

"Our friend would be most indebted to you. Performing this favor would assure you safe passage—and the most favorable terms on your future cargos."

"And what if the young lady succumbs in spite of my attentions? What if she dies under my care?"

"You'll have an easy conscience knowing you tried everything in your power to save her. And our friend will rest easier knowing everything humanly possible was done to help his beloved daughter."

The blood rushed to my head as I considered his request. I didn't want to be involved; there was so little to be done to help a laboring woman other than the customary practices employed by midwives and grannies. I was aware of Chamberlen's secret instruments, I'd read about them in the literature by Smellie and Levret, but I had nothing of the sort in my kit. I did have sugar clamps used to remove bladder stones, and these might be used in a pinch, I had been told by my late husband. Would a vapor bath be of any use? When it came to the risk of childbed, a gentlewoman was no better off than her servant. A fair number of women died giving birth, even when a medical man attended. What could I do to help her? A bleeding? A manipulation? Birthing was not my expertise. Still, I felt it my duty to at least pay a visit.

"Our friend, does he know of me? Of my surgical experience aboard ship? Does he know who I am?"

Even by candlelight I could see the twinkle in Miralles's eyes. "But of course he knows who you are. You're allowed to carry on commerce because of his good graces, not because he's blind to your presence."

How naïve of me to think I was here unnoticed by the men running Havana.

"You must know, I have very little obstetrical experience. I don't have the specialized instruments. I don't know if I can be of any help at all."

Still Miralles held my eyes. "But you'll see her tonight?"

"I'll see her as soon as I can obtain my kit."

"Thank you." He was visibly relieved. "The nuns will be expecting you. Discretion is of utmost importance, of course."

"I'm in the habit of upholding my patients' privacy. Besides, I know so few people here."

"Splendid. There's one more thing. I've heard that you're a—a fan of the masquerade." He looked away, pretending to examine the lace on his cuff.

"Meaning what, sir?"

"I've heard you're quite adept at the art of disguise."

Guyon, how much did you tell this man? I shrugged noncommittally. "What exactly are you asking me to do, sir? Please be straightforward."

"If a man is seen entering the convent, especially late at night, there will, of course, be talk. The worldly Clares are said to allow such trysts. On the other hand, if a woman is seen, there will be no eyebrows raised, no questions asked. A woman might be a family member, a servant, a nurse. A plain woman, simply dressed, wouldn't be looked at twice; females go in and out all the time."

The half-smoked cigar smoldered between my fingertips. I felt suddenly nauseated. "You want me to go dressed as a woman." It was a statement of confirmation, not a question. "But what will the nuns think? A strange woman showing up at their doorstep late at night? An English-speaking woman with a surgeon's kit in hand?"

"Leave that to me. They will be expecting you and will welcome you. If the *portera* who answers the door asks who you are, give her no name but say you are on a mission of mercy."

This was not what I had come to Havana for. It did not bode well; it could only mean trouble. But maybe nature will take care of everything. *Maybe all I have to do is be present, ask a few questions, examine the patient. The laying on of hands.*

"I must take my leave now. The instruments; I must go back to my ship."

"Of course. I'll send one of my men to fetch you." "My vessel is a two-masted tops'l schooner—"

"*Andromeda*," he interrupted. "Out of Newport. And I know where she is anchored." His lips turned up in a superior smile.

"I'll need a costume if I'm to play the part. It's not every day I'm asked to enter a nunnery in disguise." Did my host know my secret? Did Miralles think I dressed in skirts when the occasion called for it? Did he think I carried a wardrobe of disguises with me?

"You shall have something suitable to wear. My parlor maid is a leggy woman." He gave my form a swift but keen appraisal from head to toe and back again. "She's tall—nearly your height. Wait here for a moment, I'll be right back." He ground out his cigar in an ashtray on a brass stand then left me, hurrying up the balcony stairway. From somewhere on the top floor I heard a door open and shut.

A polite cough. I turned to see Guyon in the doorway, a drink in hand.

"That was quite the tête-à-tête," he said. "It seems you and Miralles have hit it off."

I was sure I had been manipulated. "I must leave the party, but don't let me interrupt your evening. I'll hire a boat."

"I wouldn't hear of it. You want to leave? I'll take you."

"You must've known about this—this situation. Why didn't you give me some warning?"

Guyon seemed genuinely puzzled. "I don't know what you're referring to. What's happened?"

"If you don't know—well, I'm not at liberty to discuss it."

Moments later, Miralles came clattering down the stairs with a bundle of blue cloth under his arm.

"You're leaving as well, Monsieur Guyon?"

Guyon nodded. "We came together. It's been a pleasure. Thank you for your hospitality, Juan."

"The pleasure is all mine, Olivier," Miralles said. Then, turning away from Guyon, he spoke with quiet urgency to me. "Expect my boat at your vessel within the hour. The man will know nothing except he is to take a woman from the Yankee ship to the shore. A servant boy will meet you at the dock and escort you to the Santa

Clara convent. All the boy knows is that you are visiting one of the Sisters, bringing her something from the outside. Tea, perhaps. A bottle of wine. Perhaps if you have a bundle or a basket with you. Something from your galley, perhaps?"

I took the bundle of cloth he offered and put it under my arm. "I'll do everything I can, sir—but don't expect a miracle."

"You are an instrument of God. If there is to be a miracle it will be because God wills it. *Vaya con Dios*, MacPherson."

If God had ever accompanied me anywhere I'd not been aware of it. Luck—both good and bad—had proven a more constant companion. If fortune's Wheel was still on the upswing I'd arrive at the convent to find the baby safely born, suckling at his mother's breast.

Giving my host a nod of acquiescence, I hurried down the stairs to the courtyard's gate, cursing Guyon under my breath.

The night was sullen and still. There was no breeze, forcing Guyon to row. He took off his coat, unbuttoned his waistcoat, rolled up his sleeves, and went to work, pulling us speedily through the water.

"What exactly have you told these men? I feel you have misrepresented me." I sat facing him, the bundle Miralles had given me pressed between my knees.

"I told them what I know." He leaned toward me, his back straight, and then pulled the oars soundlessly through the water with a long, powerful stroke.

"And what is that? What do you know about me?"

"I know what I've seen. You're a merchantman from Rhode Island, formerly a skilled surgeon who served the British Navy. I told them you're capable of assuming different identities."

Now I was forced to laugh. "Well, that's one way of describing me. Did you know I was going to be asked to help a mutual friend?"

"No, but it sounds intriguing. As we say in my country, wherever there is intrigue you can be certain a woman is involved."

"In this case, barely a woman," I said. "Little more than a girl."

"In these hot climes, girls come of age quickly. Like tropical flowers, they bloom early." He rowed on, the oars barely making a sound. "It appears that Miralles has seen how he can be repaid for what I've asked for on your behalf. He's quick to recognize such things and doesn't hesitate to ask a favor."

"What have you asked for on my behalf?"

"Exactly what you came for, my dear. A quick and profitable trade for your goods. What has he asked of you?"

"As I said before, If you don't know, I'm not at liberty to tell you."

"Can I be of assistance?"

"What can you tell me about Santa Clara?"

"The convent? It's the wealthiest in the Caribbean. They own many ranches and plantations."

"How?"

"Investments. From money given to them by their benefactors. Dowries and bequests."

"Who are their benefactors?"

"The prestigious families of Havana. The Clares provide safekeeping for their unmarried daughters until good matches can be made. Also for their aging aunts and spinsters. Sometimes for those unfortunates who find themselves *enceinte* without a husband. Sad accounts, but inside the convent walls they find a refuge. If they are of pure Spanish blood, of course."

Guyon rowed on, effortlessly, in the warm, still night.

"The manner in which they live here in Havana is quite different than the way of the founding Clares of Assisi, who lived as mendicants. Here the Clares keep personal servants and entertain guests, who bring in gifts of wine and cheese. I'm told they don't always wear their habits, but who can blame them in this heat? Decadent, some say. Wastrels. Far more indulgent than the Dominicans or the Carmelites."

"If I had to take vows and live in a religious community, it sounds like Havana's Santa Clara convent would be my choice. I've never excelled at deprivation."

"Or taking orders either, I would imagine."

We approached *Andromeda*, dark now but for the glow of a cigar on deck. Cyrus, keeping anchor watch. I hailed him, said good night to Guyon, and climbed aboard.

"I've been ashore making arrangements for our cargo," I said to Cyrus. "I have to go back on an urgent matter. Someone is coming for me shortly and I'll likely be gone the rest of the night. If our cargo arrives before I return, take delivery. Inspect the goods and hold them accountable."

Cyrus didn't say anything, but I knew he was curious. "Oh—and I'll be in disguise. I'll explain later," I said. "There's no time now."

Below in my cabin, I stripped off my waistcoat and stock, and then stepped into the dress, pulling it up over my breeches and shirt, reaching behind to fasten what hooks I could reach, leaving the rest open. My breasts did nothing to fill out the bodice but my broad shoulders strained the seams. I tied the apron around my waist, the bonnet under my neck, flung the shawl around my shoulders and fumbled to fasten it at the neck. Oh, and there in the apron pocket, the parlor maid's crumpled handkerchief. Curious, I pulled it out. Trimmed with a bit of lace and embroidered with a red G, surrounded by a ring of tiny rosebuds. Wrinkled—but clean— it smelled of lavender water. I held it to my nose and sniffed. The maid's kerchief, such a simple thing, snagged my heart. It embodied some quality, some feminine appreciation I had lost somewhere along the way in my quest to become a man.

Hearing the plash and drip of oars and the bump of a boat alongside, I stuffed the kerchief into the bodice of the borrowed gown, grabbed my instrument kit and hurried on deck, nearly bumping into Cyrus in the companionway. He looked at me, stunned.

"Stop your gawking, Cyrus. I told you I'll explain everything later. Hand this down to me." I thrust my instrument box at him and, lifting my skirts above my knees, climbed nimbly over the rail and down into the waiting boat.

Eight

Santa Clara Convent

The servant left me at the service entrance of the Santa Clara convent, a sprawling stone fortress not far from the pier. I lifted the door's iron knocker and let it fall.

A pair of eyes at the peep slit. A rattling of keys, a creaking of hinges as the door opened a crack, revealing a shaft of light and the scent of burning whale oil.

"I believe I am expected." I held up my medical kit and adjusted the bonnet on my head, feeling awkward and ugly in my costume. It had been years since I had dressed as a woman; I no longer felt at home in the clothes, skirts swishing about my legs, bodice constricting my stomach and lungs, limiting my movements.

The door opened wider to admit me and I stepped inside.

The *portera*, a tall woman whose face was hidden behind a veil, motioned for me to follow her and set off at a brisk pace down a dark gallery, the lantern swinging with every step, as if aboard ship, casting shadows on the old limestone walls. As I hurried to keep up I breathed in the damp, mineral smell and couldn't help but think of the crypt somewhere below, where the bones of dead nuns rested. Death was a palpable presence all around.

Had it not been for my guide I would have soon been lost in the maze of corridors. We hurried by closed doors, behind which I heard murmurs of voices, music, and laughter—all evidence of what I had heard about the wealthy Clares of Havana. We climbed a long narrow stairway to another long hallway, and at the end she stopped in front of a door and knocked. An aproned servant girl opened the door and motioned me inside.

This was no rude little cell but a two-room apartment, elegantly furnished. I breathed in the smell of bodies, of women's perspiration and secretions—and of fear. One small window high on the wall was open to the night air, but I could feel no breeze here. Hot as an oven.

In the bedchamber, against the far wall, was a four-poster bed, its curtains drawn closed for privacy. Two girls stood by the bed, clutching their rosaries. They were in a state of undress, wearing only long white chemises and cotton night caps over short-cropped hair. Novitiates, I supposed. Their eyes flew to me in dreadful expectation, or perhaps supplication. As if I were the Savior—or Satan.

Then a nun stepped out of the shadows to greet me, a singular woman dressed in full habit of white cloth, a cross hanging like an anchor from her neck. Only her face was visible—a mature face, serene. The mother superior, I presumed, though I knew little of the Catholic hierarchy or the proper title to address her by.

"You are the doctor I was told would come." She showed no surprise that I was a woman. Or perhaps she believed I was a man in disguise, so that no tongues would wag. Who knows what she had been told. In any case, I was glad someone in the room spoke my language.

"I am a surgeon, though I have worked under a physician. With your permission, sister, I'll examine the patient to see if there is anything I can do."

"I am the abbess, doctor. Madre Cecilia. Pull aside the bed curtains," she instructed the novitiates.

Let the play begin, I thought. There, on the bed, a mound of an abdomen, two bare legs. A woman at her side—servant or midwife, I knew not—dipped a cloth into a basin of water and wrung it out. The laboring woman's face was white and round as the moon. I was struck by how young she looked, and how close to death. Her pale lips parted; she panted softly like a dog after the chase. She seemed completely unaware of my presence. Unaware of any of us. I moved aside a birthing chair and stepped over a scattering of damp, bloody rags to get to the bedside.

The abbess spoke, a prayer or a benediction. "May the saints be with you. May God see fit to bless you in your efforts to deliver this child."

Which child was to be delivered, I wondered? A child giving birth to a child, it seemed to me.

"Does she speak English?" I asked.

"A little, yes. I'll act as translator, if need be," the abbess said. "Let me know how else we may be of assistance."

My own heart pounding hard, I leaned over the patient, feeling her hot breath on my cheek.

"Can you hear me? I'm the surgeon; I've been asked to examine you."

She looked at me, her eyes trying to focus on my face, but she made no attempt to speak. Her florid cheek was hot and dry, her lips and eyelids were swollen. I took her wrist to evaluate her pulse when a pain seized her. She moaned softly as her belly, protruding beneath the linen shift, went rigid. But the contraction did not last more than a few seconds.

"How long has she been laboring?"

"I was alerted very early this morning. Nearly twenty hours now, I would say. We have been praying to Santa Ana, San Gerardo, and Santa Maria to intercede for the young doña's strength and the infant's deliverance."

"Is there a midwife in attendance? A nurse?" I groped for the

Spanish word. "*¿La comadrona? ¿Partera?*"

One of the sisters standing by looked at me and nodded.

"Maria is one of our lay nurses, trained in the arts of midwifery," the madre said. "Her English is not so good."

"Has the patient begun to bear down? Is her cervix dilated?" I made an O with my thumbs and middle fingers.

The abbess translated and I impatiently waited for the response. "Maria says her waters broke many hours ago and the cervix is ripe but the babe's head is not engaged. She has tried everything she knows to turn the infant, but to no avail. It refuses to be born."

"Please, Madre Cecilia, kindly tell the patient I'm here to help her. Ask her if I might examine her. If I might intervene."

God, how I hated the whole business of childbirth. Painfully inconvenient at best; protracted and deadly at worst. And what relief did I have to offer? Precious little. This poor girl was beyond exhaustion. She showed signs of toxemia, one of the most severe complications. Puffy hands and legs, bounding pulses, a decreased level of consciousness.

Opening my kit, I brought out the tourniquet and bleeding bowl. But she was so swollen I could neither see nor feel a vein to let blood. Engorged as a tick.

"Has she been steamed?" I said.

The abbess conferred with the nurse. "Yes, doctor. Steamed with oil of lavender, followed by a decoction of basil and sword bean."

I had no idea what sword bean was nor what it was supposed to do. "Take that pillow away. Lie her flat."

The laboring girl groaned as the sisters did my bidding.

"Bend her knees and hold her legs apart, if you please."

I lifted the chemise, damp and stained with amniotic fluid, to reveal the hard dome of her abdomen, the glistening thatch of hair beneath, the swollen labia, dark purple in the candlelight. Placing my hands on either side of the navel, I pushed down, feeling for the head. A trickle of blood-tinged fluid dribbled out, staining the bedsheet beneath her. There it was, high and to the right side, a transverse lie, the worst possible presentation. In spite of the closeness in the room a cold sweat broke out on my forehead. I pressed down again on the right side, lifting on the left, in an effort to externally manipulate the head downward. She moaned softly and I saw between her open legs a gush of blood soak into the sheet beneath her. Slipping three fingers into the birth canal, I reached for the cervix and found it fully dilated but blocked by what felt like the placenta. *Placenta previa*—the placenta had detached from the uterine wall and was covering the cervix. The blood on my arm convinced me the umbilical cord was detaching prematurely. The unborn child hadn't long to live—in fact, it might already be dead. And the mother soon to follow.

I knew what I had to do, but it was a procedure I had never before done, nor had any surgeon I had ever known performed it. Yet I felt certain it was her only chance to live—and certainly the baby was running out of time.

Julius Caesar was delivered successfully by knife. Aeneas had once told me about a quick-thinking Swiss sow gelder who saved both his wife and infant with the knife, and a midwife, one Mary Dunally, somewhere in the north of Ireland, did safely deliver a woman using a shaving razor, closing the incision with silk thread from her sewing basket. Amazingly, the mother had lived, though the infant succumbed. There were other stories, unconfirmed, of successful Caesarian deliveries, and more of desperate butcheries that failed. Mine would be no butchery. There was a chance.

"Madre Cecilia, I must resort to extreme measures." My bonnet slipped off my shorn head, falling down my back, held only by the knot under my chin. I ripped it off and wiped the sweat from my brow with it. "The procedure itself might finish her, but I believe if she is not delivered immediately, she will die nonetheless, and soon. As will the child."

The abbess's eyes were wide, her once serene face now alarmed. "Surely you're not going to cut her open? No, there must be something else you can do. Some herb, some cathartic you can administer."

"I'm a surgeon, not an apothecary, and there is nothing else I can do that will make a damn bit of difference to mother or child. This thing must be done and it must be done now or else we stand here helpless and watch them both die."

"She is in God's hands. Our Father in heaven and his angels are waiting to receive her. The viaticum has been administered."

"Pray to heaven, Madre Cecilia; pray all you want. But her earthly father—your benefactor—has asked me to see what I can do. I am here at his request, because of his love for her. Because I am a surgeon. It's all I have to offer."

The girl stiffened and began to twitch. Her eyes rolled up into her head and her limbs began to shake violently in the uncontrolled seizures of eclampsia. The women's voices rose in chant as they prayed louder, stepping farther away from the bed in their fear. The girl's face turned red, the whites of her eyes went red with blood, and blood-speckled foam formed at the corners of her mouth. Instinctively, I grabbed the rosary on her pillow, wrapped my handkerchief around the crucifix, and slid it into her mouth to keep her from lacerating her own tongue.

"Will you assist me?" I demanded of the abbess. "I cannot do this alone. Nor can I stand by and watch her die."

The seizure was beginning to pass. The violent tremors slowed, her body became flaccid, and she made postictal snoring sounds, as if asleep.

The abbess crossed herself and gathered her resolve. "We will assist you. Tell us what to do."

"I need the nurse to hold back tissue with these." I picked up the retractors and thrust them at the nurse, who took them reluctantly. "And I need someone—you, *madre*—to soak up pooled blood with this gauze so that I can visualize the muscle." I picked up a pledget with forceps and held it out to the abbess. "Can you do it?"

Her eyes met mine and I knew she could. She reached for the forceps. The others had gathered around the bedside once again, looking like a choir of angels in their white chemises. Their smooth hands pressed together at their hearts, in anguish or in prayer, I knew not. I glanced at my own hands, freckled brown and wrinkled well before their time, yet I trusted them. These hands that could never master an embroidery needle were skilled at delving into hot, bleeding flesh and finding a torn artery, practiced at pulling catgut through severed flesh. These hands, these eyes, this brain.

Automatically assembling the other instruments at the foot of the bed, I envisioned the steps. Speed was of the essence. Speed and a sure but delicate hand. I threaded the needle with a length of catgut.

"More light, please. You girls, sisters, bring candles, quickly. And clean muslin for pledgets, I don't have enough. And fresh water, please." I looked across the bed at the abbess, ashen-faced but standing tall, forceps in hand, waiting to assist. "What is this young woman's name?"

All about us the sisters were scurrying to fetch what I had asked for. The abbess, sworn to protect the young doña's reputation and privacy, met my eyes but was reluctant tell me.

"Please, *madre*, I must know her name. I must have her consent if I am to do this."

"Theresa."

"Theresa," I repeated. The crucifix had fallen from her mouth onto the bed. She slept in a state of exhaustion. I felt her brow, hot and dry. I smoothed the dark hair back from her face, tucking it behind her ears. I pressed lightly on her sternum. "Theresa!"

Her eyes fluttered open. She looked at me with an equanimity that unsettled me, focused on something or someone above my right shoulder. An unseen saint or angel? I hoped if it were an angel that it would guide my hand.

"Do you hear me? Can you understand my words?"

She nodded, almost imperceptibly.

"Theresa, do you object to me cutting into your womb to deliver this infant? There are great risks involved and you may die from complications. But I fear you will die if I do not do it."

"*Sí*," she whispered. "*Socorro. Por favor.*" And then she slipped back into unconsciousness, her lips slightly parted, her eyes half open.

Soon a dozen lanterns cast a warm light onto the bed and a sound of voices, female voices murmuring in unison, buoyed me, encouraged me. In my mind's eye, I could picture the anatomy; I knew what I had to do.

"Let's go!" My voice was a thunderclap. "Bear a hand now, I need your help. All of you. Hold her knees, her arms, lest she kick involuntarily. Maria, Madre Cecilia—you two will stand by to assist me."

I made the first cut above where I knew the bladder was, revealing the yellow adipose tissue and the dark, hard moon of the uterus. Blood seeped around my hands as I pulled back the skin and the fat. I bade the nurse to retract it while I palpated again to determine the fetus's position. The abbess sponged away the blood and I made a longitudinal cut through the fibrous uterine wall, surprising tough, I thought. No turning back now. Laying my scalpel down, I reached into the pulsating organ and with some effort drew forth the limp blue legs of a girl child, manipulating gently until I freed her head, matted with a pelt of black hair. To my great relief the slippery mass of flesh squirmed in my hands. Alive, alive!

Holding her on my left hand and arm, I swept her mouth clear of fluid with the index finger of my right hand, willing her to breathe. Breathe! A gasp, followed by a weak, mewling cry heartened me and did much to improve her color. *Go on, cry; scream bloody hell*, I willed, handing the slippery babe to the nurse, along with the warm, blue placenta attached to the umbilical cord.

"Please see to the infant."

Now to save the mother. The uterus was beginning to contract, a good sign. I picked up the needle and catgut and closed the incision, leaving long ends so the stitches might be removed in a week, should she live that long. With good nursing care, the catgut would hold, the tissue would granulate and heal, though scarring was unavoidable. What she would tell some future husband on some future wedding night about that telltale scar, I had not a care. I only hoped she would live to see morning's light, which was fast approaching.

"Bring more dressings, please. And wine," I said to the abbess. "Madre Cecilia, she needs good red wine and warm marrow broth by the spoonful."

"Theresa." I took her hand in mine, her warm living hand. Still swollen but squeezing mine in return. The radial pulse was rapid and weak, but it was a pulse. "Can you hear me?"

Her thick black lashes fluttered. She opened her eyes but stared past me, as if looking at someone over my shoulder. I had seen that look before.

"Your child is delivered, a baby girl. She lives. Now you must live too." Did I imagine the pressure on my hand by those frail fingers? "Did you hear me, Theresa? *Vive. ¡Vive!*"

Gathered around the bed, the women began to talk in hushed voices, prayer beads in hand. Their voices in unison sounded to me like the ringing of bells. Silver bells.

Santa María, Madre de Dios
Llena eres de gracia
El Señor es contigo
Bendita tú eres entre todas las mujeres...

I dressed the incision with a thick pad of muslin, tying it in place with strips of cloth, and then washed my hands in the basin of water, staining it red. The nurse brought the infant, rooting and squirming, to the bedside, saying something in Spanish. The abbess translated. "She should be put to suckle. There won't be milk yet, but the first fluid is good and the instinct is strong."

Seeing the rosary on the bed, I took the handkerchief from the crucifix. Folded it, still damp with her spittle and stained with her blood. Stowed it away under the bodice of my dress, between my own breasts, wet with perspiration.

My work done, I stood aside as the nurse took over, handing the swaddled bundle to the young mother, who reached out in bewilderment. I watched as the baby nuzzled blindly against the mother's dumpling of a breast, the nurse pinching the wide, dark nipple, guiding it into the gaping pink mouth. Wondrous, how that mouth knew what to do. I felt I had just taken part in a performance, a play. I was a stand-in, an understudy, thrust into a role I wasn't prepared for. Yet I had memorized the lines, I knew the stage directions, I had done my best, and now the curtain was coming down on the second act. There was no applause. But someone brought me a chair, and I sank into it, relieved.

Church bells tolled five. Dawn. Voices singing in unison. I had drifted off to sleep. Opened my eyes to see the child mother, still breathing, the sleeping babe in the crook of her bare arm.

So many infants died in their first year of life. So many of their mothers died giving birth, and many more in the days immediately following. But right now, at this second hour postpartum, these two, mother and daughter, breathed. I watched their chests rise and fall, nearly imperceptible movements that sustained life. Breath *was* life. I held my own in wonder.

Outside the window, beyond the enclosure, the city came to life.

A servant of the nuns brought me coffee, good strong Cuban coffee—life's blood!—sweetened with milk and sugar to revive me, and a slice of bread with jam. The nurse brought me the newborn for my inspection. She had passed her first stool. She had been cleaned and was pink now, with good muscle tone. She looked at my face with black eyes, unfocused but bright. Such a tiny thing, five or six pounds, legs kicking now. I marveled at her delicate ears and lips, the little squashed nose, the unruly hair. I touched her cheek gently with my rough, red finger and marveled as she turned toward it to suckle. I nearly wept.

Guyon was waiting with Miralles's servant boy just beyond the convent gate. He escorted me quickly through the streets, busy with water boys and hucksters, to his waiting boat and rowed me out against the tide. As soon as we were offshore I lay on the bottom of the boat under the cover of a sail and wiggled out of the dress, revealing my sweat-soaked breeches and shirt beneath. I rolled up the gown, the bonnet, and the shawl for Guyon to return to Miralles. The soiled handkerchief, I kept.

"I've just come from your ship," Guyon said. "You'll be pleased to know your cargo has been delivered and is all accounted for. I managed to obtain a dozen cigars, for goodwill." He smiled and handed me an envelope. "A false invoice, should you need it."

As we approached *Andromeda,* I could see Cyrus and the men on deck making ready for departure, stowing water barrels and securing the ship's boat. Guyon pulled up alongside, barely grazing the schooner's starboard hull.

"Ahoy, captain," George called, tossing down a dock line for us.

"This is for you, from our mutual friend," Guyon said, placing a cloth sack in my palm. English wool; I knew its hand well. Dark blue, cut from a sailor's jacket sleeve and tied at the neck with a strip of leather. "A token of his appreciation. He wishes you Godspeed and hopes you'll return."

I could feel the heft and the movement of the coins inside the sack; thick heavy coins sliding against each other, nestling into the palm of my hand. It seemed crass to look inside to count them, but by the weight I judged it to be a considerable amount. I slipped it into my pocket. Would she live? For how long? At what point was I absolved of my responsibility? A surgeon's pay isn't based on outcome, and we all die in the end.

Guyon must've read my thoughts. "Life is a risk, is it not? You are sailing for Rhode Island and I for New Orleans. Godspeed to us both. Let us meet here in the spring. April?"

"I don't know; how can I know? We never really discussed particulars." I was anxious now to be done with this place, to be on my way. "I have partners and shareholders I'm accountable to. I'll likely be back, yes—with more rum, and horses too, if I can get them. Narragansett pacers are in great demand."

"What I trade in commands a good price and takes up absolutely no space in the hold. Remember that, my friend."

"I don't think I'm very good at this, Guyon."

"I beg to differ. Please, write me at this address." He handed me a folded piece of paper, closed with a seal. "All the particulars are in the letter."

I climbed aboard.

"*Au revoir*, Patrick."

His upturned face, a quick smile, a touch of his hat, and then he pushed off with an oar and I looked away, tucking the letter inside my breast pocket.

Nine

December 18, 1765
At Sea

The winds had been contrary, the return passage longer than expected, but I was twenty Spanish dollars richer—not including my share of the voyage profits, most of which I planned to reinvest in the partnership. That and a new pair of shoes.

Every man aboard looked forward to the payoff and shore time. Even Moses and Sam stood to profit. They had been hired out by Dominic but would receive a good percentage of the wage. We were a shorthanded merchant ship, overworked and low on stores, but we were a happy ship just then, everyone in high spirits, readying the ship to make port.

"Hard to believe we were miserably hot a fortnight ago." Cyrus pulled his cap down over red-tipped ears and rubbed his hands together briskly. He and I were enjoying a few minutes of company on deck together in the late afternoon, the day before landfall.

My hands were still raw from my last trick at the helm—cracked and bleeding now from the cold, having only recently healed from sunburn and salt sores. I cradled the coffee mug in my palms, glad for the comforting warmth.

"Maybe you'd like to borrow the kid gloves I bought in Havana for my sister?" Cyrus teased.

He had been ribbing me about women's clothing ever since seeing me leave the ship that night dressed in skirts and a bonnet. I had told him I went to a masquerade ball but I said it in jest, and he knew it. More than once I had seen him looking at me in a certain way, like he was trying to decide if what crossed his mind might actually be true. But the idea that a woman could command a ship, even a small merchant ship such as *Andromenda*, was so out of the ordinary, he probably never properly formed the question even in his mind. He wouldn't challenge me—at least I hoped he wouldn't. And maybe I just imagined his suspicion. Maybe it was my own doubts and fears I projected onto him. Earlier in the voyage he had seemed anxious for me to meet his sister, to court her. He took me for a red-blooded man then, so why shouldn't he now?

"Gloves? Now there's a luxury," I said.

"Riding gloves, a gift for Juliana. Made of Spanish kid."

"Your sister will be delighted, I'm sure. And just in time for Christmas."

"She's an excellent horsewoman. You have to visit us sometime and go riding with her. I'll wager she'll put you through the paces."

"That reminds me, have you any horses for sale? There's money to be made on fine carriage horses. I intend to take as many as I can on the next run."

He grinned disarmingly. "I'm a waterman, Patrick, not a ploughman. I know nothing of horses. I gave up my birthright to the farm."

I would've liked to know more about Cyrus. I liked him. I would have enjoyed getting to know him better. But my pretense prohibited the intimacy of friendship, as did my role as captain. I had to keep most everyone at a distance. I had enjoyed those few hours with Rachel and I had enjoyed the attentions of Guyon. That would have to suffice for now. But eventually, when I had enough money, I could … what?

"We should be raising Block's Island soon," I said, chewing on rum-soaked coffee grounds and looking westward. It had been a slow trip, with the winds, but I had clear skies often enough to plot our position quite accurately. I was confident we would be home by tomorrow night.

"Is the plan still to off-load at Mr. Eli's plantation?"

I nodded. "Those were my instructions. We'll stick by them." I didn't want to risk Newport, where a warship might be waiting to harass us. Who knew if anything had changed in the weeks we'd been gone? It had been a successful run so far, my first voyage as captain; I didn't want to chance ruining it now.

"The boys are happy; they're about to be paid off and they've made a little profit on their own adventures."

"And you, Cyrus? Was it a good voyage for you?"

Again, the carefree, cocky grin. "One more night ashore would have been better. So many lovelies in Havana, of every shade and hue. Next time…"

"You stay too long, you get a fever," I bantered.

"Too late, sir. I believe I already have."

"I have some calomel and bark aboard; I'd be happy to dose you."

Cyrus lowered his voice to a more confidential tone. "Can I ask you something, Patrick—something personal?"

Oh, here it comes. And what shall I say? I'll take offense and strike him down. I'll laugh it off, friendly banter. But what if I owned up to it?

"Fire away," I said lightly, my own heart firing away in my chest.

"That last night in Havana when I saw you. In disguise. As a woman."

I forced a patient, indulgent smile. "You saw me in costume, yes, Cyrus. I was called upon to do a favor for a—an acquaintance."

His eyes searched my face and I maintained the mask, smiling blandly. "I hope you were successful."

I nodded. "I was. But that's all I'm at liberty to say."

His turn to nod. "It's just I've sometimes wondered. When I came to your rescue—your assistance—after you were swept overboard on the outbound passage and were clinging to the rail, I—"

"A very timely intervention. I'm deeply grateful, Cyrus," I said, interrupting him, yet holding his blue gaze, reading everything in his eyes. I knew then that he knew. "Let us put the matter at rest, shall we?" I managed a dismissing smile.

"As you wish, Patrick. You're the captain."

Ten

Off Block Island

"Land ho! And a ship to windward," George called from the bow. "Looks like a frigate."

I went to the rail, raised my glass. There on the horizon, a bit of white sail blended in with the whitecaps.

"On a course to intercept us, it appears," I said to Cyrus, who came bounding up the companionway, followed by Moses and Sam.

Maybe they were just headed to Newport. Maybe they weren't interested in us. I climbed a few rungs of the ratlines to have a better look. My stomach churned at the sight of it, hull up from this vantage point. Oh, they were interested, to be sure.

"Let's press on and see if we can give them the slip."

"They have the wind," Cyrus said.

"I'm well aware of that. We can't outrun them on this tack, but close to the island when the wind drops, our schooner has the advantage. You're the local pilot, Cyrus. Can we evade them? Hide out in shallow water?"

His jaw worked for a moment as he studied the horizon, and then he went below to look at the chart.

"There may be more wind aloft. Set the fisherman stays'l and trim the sheets; let's milk every bit of speed we can," I said to the men "We should be able to make six knots."

I took a sun sight and went below to plot it. We were still at least thirty nautical miles from the mouth of the Narragansett, but Block's Island, just ahead, offered us an escape. When I came back up on deck the frigate was hull up, and still on a course to intercept us.

"There, the Mohegan Bluffs," I said to Cyrus. "Let's see if we can point a little higher into the wind without losing speed. Cross the frigate's bow and make for the west side of Block's Island."

"It's risky. We'll lose the wind as we approach the island. Or it will shift. But that could be to our advantage."

"You have the tiller, Mr. Lovelace. Coax her closer to the wind, as close as she will go. George, you and Moses on the sheets—main and fore. Keep her trimmed constantly; it's teamwork we're needing now. Sam, you handle the stays'ls and I'll keep us apprised of their relative position."

My gamble was that the frigate wouldn't be able to hold the new course. If we could reach the shallow waters off Block's Island, we might have a chance to evade her completely. We all knew what was at stake and we were determined not to be easy prey; we'd give them a run for it. The men were diligent on the sheets, tightening and easing with each variance in the wind's strength, their ability to read the pattern of wind on the water helping them to anticipate a gust or a drop. Our fore-and-aft sails allowed us more maneuverability, but still the ship gained on us, growing larger, looming like a frigate bird swooping down on its prey.

Minutes passed. Quarter hours. I turned the glass at the binnacle and struck the bell to mark the passage of time. I was aware now of the raw New England chill gnawing at my bones. I thought of the hogsheads of Spanish sugar stowed tightly below. Ahead, the island rose ever so slowly out of the gray sea and Cyrus steered for the shallow waters, hoping to make it before the warship bore down upon us.

We beat into the wind, heeled over, swells breaking on our larboard bow, the sails taut as drumheads. I stood next to Cyrus on the tiller.

"What's your plan?" he asked, his jaw tight.

"Grace Cove, on the west side of the island."

He nodded. "I know it well."

"They won't be able to follow us into the cove."

"No." He frowned. "But she can blow us out of the water like a sitting duck."

"Not if they lose sight of us. We're losing daylight. After dark, we definitely have the advantage."

My mate studied the horizon, the sun already low in the sky. These were the short December days just before the solstice.

"So," I said, "unless you have a better plan, how can we make this happen?"

"There's a narrow break in North Reef; it's quite close to shore. The frigate won't risk it, I'm certain. Though it's the time of year for the Palatine light to appear; maybe the ghosts will work in our favor and serve as a decoy for us."

He was probably jesting, though I couldn't be certain. In Rhode Island, belief in the ghostly phenomenon of Block's Island was strong.

The Palatine light was a reference to the apparition, and the story varied with the telling. One version I heard suggested it was a ghost ship—a ship in flames that haunted the waters on the north end of the island every year around Christmastime. Another version said the light was a malevolent force in the form of a false beacon, to lure ships to their doom on Sandy Point, the northern tip of the reef, where a ship of German Palatine immigrants was wrecked back in 1738. The voyage had been plagued with bad luck—or bad management—from the start, the story went, with half the crew, the captain, and two hundred passengers dying from tainted water before a storm drove them onto Sandy Point. I had first heard about it from Dominic Hale, who most decidedly did not believe in ghosts yet always gave the north reef a wide berth.

"I don't believe in ghosts, Cyrus. And neither does the captain of that frigate, I assure you. But I most definitely believe in shipwrecks and I don't want to be counted among all the bones that certainly lie at the base of that reef. You say you're familiar with this passage? And you're certain we can navigate it?"

"I know it, and yes, I've made use of it many times—in a small fishing boat, not a schooner. But I think it's deep and wide enough for *Andromeda* to pass as long as the wind holds steady and we keep well to larboard. And if we're lucky. Once we're through it's just a short run along the coast to the cove."

"Then it's up to you to pilot us through. We can't allow them to board us; we'll be taken for sure. They may press our men. Even you."

"You don't need to tell me that," he snapped. "I've been taken before. This time I've got my papers with me, below in my trunk. But the others don't."

I took bearings on the island, which was growing larger by the minute, and went below to mark our position on the chart. Just beneath the water the North Reef projected half a mile beyond Sandy Point, the island's northern tip. If the frigate was intent on seizing us at sea, avoiding the sandbar would cost them time. On the other hand, they might decline a chase at this late hour and just wait to intercept us in Newport. That seemed the most likely course of action. Except we weren't going to Newport.

I went into my cabin, opened my sea chest for the pistol—not that I expected to use it, but just in case—thrust it beneath the waistband of my breeches, and hurried back on deck.

"We're crossing her bow," George said, handing me the glass.

Through it I could see the frigate's open gunports, and men on the deck. They were perhaps two hundred yards to windward. My stomach dropped upon seeing her at this range. The *Richmond*, I was almost certain.

"She's heading up, she's got gun ports open, she's running out a gun." My voice was tight in my throat. Then came the flash of fire, followed by the crack and the boom. A cannonball over the bow was a clear warning for us to heave to and wait to be boarded, yet it had the opposite effect on me. The cannon fire blew up my fear and charged me with outrage.

"Bastards," Cyrus cursed through clenched teeth. But his eyes were alight, and his face was intent.

"We've crossed their bow," George called.

"Maintain course and speed."

A gust of cold wind came up, a bit of luck for us. Our schooner was more maneuverable than the frigate; this point of sail was too close to the wind for the square-rigger. She would have to wear ship. I prayed our wind would hold favorable until we got through the break in the sandbar.

"Tighten the mains'l," I called out, but George and Moses were already in action; we were all thinking as one. Another flash of powder and resounding boom followed by a whistling sound as another cannonball flew overhead. "Make for the break, Mr. Lovelace. When we get close, I'll take the tiller and you will con us through."

Cyrus nodded. It seemed unnecessary to mention we were losing daylight fast.

"When the moon rises, we'll leave the cove and cross the sound for the west side of Narragansett Bay," I said to Cyrus. "I'm relying on you to keep us off the rocks. Can you do it?"

"I know the coastline like the deacon knows his Bible. But that won't matter if the wind is against us. Or dies completely. Let's hope Mr. Eli has a fire burning for us."

Ahead lay the reef and the bones of ships it had gathered.

"We're losing our wind," I said, feeling the change on my face and seeing the sails slacken ever so slightly. "I'll take the helm now. You go forward and con us through the break."

Moses and Sam readied the anchor cable in case the wind died. Once we entered the break, we'd be committed to passing all the way through. Like threading a needle, it would take good eyes and steady hands.

The frigate had changed course and was now out of sight, but I knew they had not given up.

"There it is," Cyrus called out from the foredeck. "I see the break, two points off the larboard bow."

"How does it look?" I called out. I could feel the current, stronger now. "Can we make it on this tack?"

He held out his left arm, indicating I should bear to larboard.

"Mind the sheets, George. Here we go." I eased the tiller, feeling the pressure of the water against the rudder as we entered the pass, hearing the rush of water against the hull. We were close to the wind, at the edge of our maneuverability. The current was running so strong through the break, it seemed we were standing still. My throat thickened, and my palms sweated in spite of the cold. Minutes dragged by, yet we seemed not to make progress. On either side, I could see the shadow of the reef beneath the surface.

"Larboard! Keep to larboard!" Cyrus yelled, pointing left and waving his arm emphatically.

The sun was low in the sky, spilling gold on the water, painting the scattered clouds pink. The sand had run through the glass, unnoticed; I dared not break my concentration to turn it over. And then the color began to fade, turning purple and then gray as *Andromeda* at last clawed her way through the gap and into deeper water. Still, my heart was in my throat until the dangerous reef was well astern.

At last Cyrus turned and grinned, raising his arms in victory, and I felt every man's relief like a great rush of air. We had navigated the pass; now, on to the cove where the waters were just deep enough to allow us shelter. The sun had disappeared, dropping behind a band of clouds on the horizon, and the wind had dropped to a whisper. Steering close to the shoreline, we ghosted along, looking for an anchorage. I could see smoke rising on shore from a few chimneys and could see the dark shapes of fishing boats dragged up on the beach. A shadow passed overhead—a night heron soaring out over the water.

After dropping anchor in shallow water—less than two fathoms here—the crew wolfed down cold johnnycakes in the dark. I did not want to risk lighting even a glim as we waited for the darkness to deepen and the moon to rise. After they had finished eating, I had George, Moses, and Sam stand down for a few hours. They would need to be rested for the night ahead of us.

Cyrus and I alone stood on deck, keeping watch for the frigate. We raised our collars and tightened our scarves against the rising wind, now from the northwest. It would be a hard beat north to Point Judith, our waypoint, just eight nautical miles across the sound. A short distance up the bay from Point Judith was an inlet, a shallow cove, where Eli had built his wharf.

"Once we've unloaded, we'll reload with some cargo from Eli's barns," I said. "Sheep and corn, local produce, whatever he's got. Then we'll head upriver to Providence. Avoid Newport altogether. Can you pilot us by moonlight?"

He nodded. "As long as the visibility remains good. I know the West Bay well."

He didn't have to say what he was thinking –that a wind change might bring a weather change. We both knew the likelihood of snow or fog, which would make a night entry impossible. Yet we dare not stay at anchor in this cove all night or we'd be a sitting duck come morning.

"The frigate has either rounded the North Reef and is making her way toward us now, or is waiting for us in Narragansett Sound," I said. "I think we should roust the men and raise anchor, not wait for moonrise; it'll be up by the time we reach the point. What do you think, Cyrus? I value your opinion."

"I think we have no time to lose."

Eleven

Narragansett Bay

A mariner's bonfire flickered on Judith Point. Apparently, we weren't the only ones coming into the West Bay. A yellow moon, one day past full, had risen above a bank of low-lying clouds to the east and was spilling its cold light onto the black water. Almost home now. Another hour and we should see Eli's welcoming fire guiding us to the wharf. A long night's work ahead yet, unloading the remaining barrels in the dark. With any luck, we'd all be having Christmas dinner at a Newport tavern. I wondered if the Redbone brig had returned yet.

"Captain, we've got company," George said. "To the northeast, off the starboard beam."

Looking over my shoulder I saw it, a shadow in the distance. Silent as an owl in flight.

"Mr. Lovelace, can you find us a hiding place?"

Cyrus thought for a minute, staring out into the night as if was studying a chart in his head. "There's a bar on the other side of Judith Point. A salt pond to hide in. Risky at night, but..."

"It's our best option," I said, finishing his sentence. I didn't want to lead them straight to Eli's wharf, and Newport was out of the question—they might already be there, intending to intercept us. We needed to hide and our advantages were our knowledge of the local waters, our shallower draft, and our greater maneuverability.

"Do you have another plan, Cyrus? A better plan? I'm willing to hear it."

He voiced the obvious alternative: "We could turn about and run back out to sea. Try to lose them in the night."

"The frigate has the advantage of speed on nearly every point of sail. They will find us by light of day; they have nothing but time on their hands. At sea, they will hunt us down. If you can get us into that salt pond, we'll drop sail and our masts will blend in with the trees on shore. When the tide begins to ebb, the frigate won't even be able to come close."

"Of course, the riskiest part is getting through the bar—just like it was getting through the break in North Reef," Cyrus said. "The frigate has to stand off—but if they see us they can launch a boat and send it in after us."

"If they see us. I'm guessing they haven't. Not yet. Dark sails aren't nearly as visible in the moonlight."

He weighed the options. Yet I knew in my heart that the best action was the most difficult one to carry off. As captain, I alone would take the blame if we were caught. The shareholders would lose their investments and I would lose command of *Andromeda*. I did not, at that moment, consider other consequences.

"Make ready to come about," I called out.

"We're losing our wind," Cyrus muttered.

"Then let's make haste. After we come about and are on the new tack, you'll have the con again."

A rounding up of the helm through the eye of the wind brought a rattle of wooden blocks and a flap of canvas. We fell off and the wind filled our sails on the new tack. The moon, rising, lit our way with milky white light.

"There it is, captain. The break, dead ahead."

"Take us in, Mr. Lovelace."

Already we were losing our light as clouds moved in, concealing the moon. Cyrus was navigating by the sound of the water breaking on shore, by the dark shadows of trees and rocks on the land, so close. He was navigating by memory, instinct, and luck. I hoped it was enough.

"I've got it," he called from the rail to reassure me. "Maintain your course."

"Can we make it on this tack?" My knees shook, my teeth chattered.

"Yes. It appears to be nearing slack tide."

Perfect timing: the tide was on our side.

I called out, "Stand by the sheets, we're going in!"

"Ready on the sheets!" the men responded.

"On my mark, Patrick. Eight points to starboard."

I picked out a landmark, the dark shape of a distant tree on shore. "Ready on the tiller."

"Five ... four ... three ... two ... one ... Hard a-starboard!"

The sound of swishing water, the rub of hemp in blocks, the crack of sail as *Andromeda* turned toward the pass.

"Steady ... steady ..."

For a minute it was quiet but for the soft purl of water against the hull. My hand seemed to have frozen to the tiller; I could scarce feel it, numb with cold. But I kept my eye on the distant tree. Reminded myself to breathe. Prayed for more wind; we were losing our drive.

And then the sickening thump as we struck the bar. A grinding sound and sudden stop. Hard aground.

Every man felt it and knew what to do. They set to it, loosening sheets, pushing out the booms, working together to try to sail us off the sand bar. But our sails hung impotently; there was no wind to fill them and we were still hard aground. The tide was already starting to ebb and if we didn't get back afloat soon we'd be stuck on the bar for hours, until the high tide came in again.

"Starboard rail!" We all climbed outboard, hanging onto the rail, hoping our combined weight on the leeward side would be enough to float the ship again. It wasn't. The keel was lodged fast in the mud.

"Lighten the ship!" Back over the rail again, I hurried aft to the line locker, tossing coils of rope onto the deck. "George, Moses—ready the boom tackle! Cyrus, Sam—below in the hold."

We launched the boat and began hauling the barrels of molasses up, lashing them together and dropping them over the side so they might be retrieved later—an old Cornwall smuggler's trick I had heard about from my partners. We colonials didn't usually resort to such complicated subterfuge. We had longstanding arrangements with the customs officials—the former customs officials, that is, as our old friends had all been replaced by new appointees who stood to personally gain by enforcing the new duties.

In spite of the cold weather we all were working up a sweat from the physical effort of getting the barrels overboard. The men were working as fast and quietly as possible, with only the occasional grunt or word being uttered. An hour later we had sunk sixteen barrels, with an empty bottle tied to the bitter end as a buoy to mark the spot. We tried again to float *Andromeda* off but the water level was dropping as the moon passed its zenith and pulled it away. We were stuck fast.

I left to go astern for a better look into the bay and beyond. The moon broke through the clouds again, sliding into the western sky. There was the frigate, out in open water, her white sails silvery gray in the moon's pale light. She looked to be under a single topsail and staysail; the air was too light for any more canvas. The captain wouldn't risk getting his ship much closer to shore at night, in these conditions, but he had likely spotted us and he wasn't about to let us out of his sight. I was certain he meant to seize us, come the morning light.

"The frigate, they're out there, maybe half a mile away. George,

Moses—ready the anchor and kedge us off."

"And then what?" Cyrus challenged. "There's not enough wind to sail."

"We'll tow her through the pass. Back into the shallow water of the pond."

The mate shook his head stubbornly. "We'd be pulling the schooner against the tide. All the water ebbing through this channel—we'd need Hercules at the oars."

I wouldn't admit it but Cyrus was right. And even if we could get afloat in an ebbing tide, hiding inside the salt pond was to no avail if the frigate had spotted us, which seemed likely. But I was determined to get my ship unstuck and afloat again.

"Then we won't try to pull her into the pond; we'll let the tide carry us out, once we're free of the reef. We'll keep towing her, taking our turns at the oars, until we find wind and can sail. Let's get the sheet anchor in the boat and kedge off this damn sand bar. If they've seen us, and I suspect they have, they'll send a boat, an armed boat." They all stared at me as if I had lost my mind.

"Do as I say, and quickly! There's no time to lose."

Looking back, I wonder if things would have turned out differently had I not insisted on my course of action then. Had we continued to drop cargo over the side, Cyrus would have been down below, tying a line around a barrel of molasses. As it happened, George and Moses were in the boat below, preparing to receive the bow anchor suspended from the boom's block and tackle swung out over the water, while Cyrus and I were on deck, manning the halyard.

"Captain—we have visitors," Sam said, hurrying up from the stern, where he had been keeping a lookout.

"Avast." I put my hand on Cyrus's arm and held my breath, listening. A plash of water, and then another. It might have been a fish jumping but I knew better. It was the sound oars make.

Suddenly, out of the darkness, the flash and crack of musket fire. Then a voice, close at hand.

"Schooner! We are His Majesty's Royal Navy. Identify yourself."

I could see the launch now, coming up behind us, a swivel gun mounted in the bow. Men, many men, the dark shapes of muskets at the ready, rowing up alongside us.

"Schooner *Andromeda*," I called. "Out of Newport. Local traders."

"*Andromeda*, prepare to be boarded!"

I looked at Cyrus and nodded. He moved to cleat off the halyard and just as he did another shot rang out and my mate fell onto the deck, the halyard went flying—whether the anchor fell into our boat or beside it, I knew not. *My God, they've shot him—they've shot Cyrus. Surely there's some mistake.*

My shock and disbelief combined, exploding furiously. I drew my pistol and fired blindly into the gun boat, a single shot. Then I dropped to my knees beside Cyrus, who was sprawled at my feet. I lay the weapon on the deck so I would have both hands free to tend to him. Shouts, orders, a ruckus and clatter of boots and muskets, but all of my attention was on the fallen man.

His left eye stared at me in the dark. The right eye was gone, blood spurting from the dark hole where it had been. I pressed my hand against his eye socket to stop the bleeding, and felt the shattered orbital bone beneath, a warm and pulpy mess. "Stay with me, Cyrus." I placed his warm head in my lap and pulled his once fair hair, now soaked with blood, away from his face, his one-eyed stare. He didn't see me.

The wind came up again, an icy breath that found its way down my neck, clearing my head and chilling me to the bone. There on the deck I felt the life leave his body like a puff of air, to drift away on the wind. The blood continued to run warm against my thigh, but I knew he was dead. My fingers felt for a carotid pulse but there was none. No breath on my hand. Laying his head on the deck, I closed his remaining eyelid with a bloody fingertip and then stood to meet my captors.

Twelve

Aboard *Andromeda*

I recognized him even in the darkness, the way he moved as he hauled himself up over the gunwale. Four marines clambered up after him; I was aware of their bayoneted muskets trained upon me. One of them had just shot Cyrus.

"Do not resist. Drop your weapons at once."

That voice. His voice. Yes, the memory of it was forever with me.

"Do not resist and ye'll not be harmed. In the name of His Majesty's frigate *Richmond,* I place ye under arrest."

I opened my palms, sticky with Cyrus's blood, to show him I was unarmed.

"Are ye the shipmaster?"

"I am."

"How many men are aboard?"

"We are five," I said, and as soon as the words were out of my mouth I realized we were only four. And then George and Moses climbed onto the deck, surrounded by marines.

"Smith, Tibbits—search belowdecks." Then to me, "Surrender your weapons, shipmaster, or suffer the consequences."1

"But you shot my first mate," I roared. "You killed him!"

"Shut your mouth and hand me your firearms or ye'll be shot too, I promise ye."

"My pistol, it's there on the deck. I have no other weapon; we're traders. Since when does the navy attack her own people, Brian Dalton?" I was aware of my bare head—what had become of my hat, I wondered? I felt a prickling of my scalp staring down the barrels of those muskets at the ready.

"Who are ye?" he growled, taking a wider stance. "How do ye know my name?"

"I'm Patrick MacPherson, master of this vessel."

I felt the shock of his recognition, as if he had been punched in the gut. I felt the air rush out of him.

"Patrick MacPherson?" His voice was hard but I heard the crack in it. I felt a small, strange rush of gratitude that he did not instantly expose me. He was capturing me on my terms, as a man. Yet had I been exposed as a woman, events might have turned out very differently.

"Patrick MacPherson," I repeated. "The very same." We looked at each other by the light of the moon, half hidden as it dropped into a bank of clouds in the western sky. My old friend and lover, a body's length away. For a moment it was just the two of us, in another place and time.

"Ye took up with the Yankees," he said.

"And you have killed my man." The words poured forth now; I was quite unable to stop them. The anger, the outrage boiled up. "You chased us without cause, you hunted us down, and now you have shot and killed my man, an innocent mariner. For what reason? On whose authority?"

"I'm under orders to seize your vessel and take ye into custody. Hand over your papers and no one else gets hurt," he added. I sensed his conflict.

By now, three more marines had climbed aboard and surrounded us in a circle, like some absurd children's game, while the blood of Cyrus Lovelace pooled at their feet. I trembled—from fear, from rage, or from the bitter Narragansett wind that now blew steady, I knew not. The little world I had worked so hard to build was cracked and bleeding, and this long-awaited reunion with my former shipmate was not at all how I dreamed it would be. A living nightmare, this.

I pulled the false invoice from my breast pocket and handed it to him, our fingers brushing in the dark. The invoice wouldn't pass muster but it just might buy me time. But Brian didn't bother to look at the papers, stuffing them away inside his coat instead. All the while, his eyes were locked on mine, as if he was trying to convey something to me. Or maybe he just couldn't believe what I had become. A Yankee smuggler, he would call me. A mariner, a merchant captain, I called myself. We always did see things differently. I don't know how or why we ever liked each other— much less loved.

Dalton was always slow to speak; a man of few words but not a man to be trifled with. Even though my ship had just been taken and Cyrus lay dead on the deck, I felt the strange attraction between us like some sort of phenomenon of nature, like Saint Elmo's fire.

When he spoke again, it was firmly, with full measure and the intention of a British naval officer. "Ye ignored our signals to heave to; ye deliberately evaded us. Now ye have shot and wounded my lieutenant. This vessel and its contents are seized and ye are under arrest, Patrick MacPherson, as master of this vessel."

I felt alone and betrayed, yet I knew I must not give up. I knew I must make a connection, must look to save what was left of my crew, must look to save my ship.

"Your lieutenant, Mr. Dalton, the wounded officer—is it Mr. Mason?" Young Mason was the first lieutenant when I served *Richmond* as surgeon's mate. A good man and a fine officer.

"No, not Mason; he has his own command now. Lieutenant Markham. He has been hit in the shoulder."

"How far away is the frigate?"

"Quite close," he equivocated.

"Your lieutenant needs attention now. Bring him aboard, I'll treat him. You know I have the skills."

"I know all too well." Then to his men he barked, "Bring Mr. Markham onto the schooner, we have a surgeon onboard."

"If you'll allow my men to rig the boom and sling…"

"Do it."

Muskets still pointed at them, George and Moses prepared the tackle to hoist the wounded officer up on deck, while one marine accompanied me as I went below to ready my tools and the galley table.

Thirteen

Aboard *Andromeda*

Markham was a young officer, about my own age, and no doubt eager to make his mark by seizing my ship and to collect his share of the proceeds. Having served aboard the frigate, having earned a share of prize money myself once, I understood his motivation. I couldn't hold any anger toward the young lieutenant; on the contrary, I felt sympathy for him and a growing sense of horror that I was the one who had wounded him. I was the one who had drawn the pistol, cocked it, and pulled the trigger. I had shot him defending my men and my ship, but that didn't alter the fact that Cyrus was dead. An eye for an eye was no settlement at all. I had not heard an order; I didn't even know if it was the lieutenant who had ordered the firing. I didn't remember taking aim. The shooting had been automatic and instinctive. Now I set about caring for the wound I had inflicted. This was work I knew how to do.

In the warmth of *Andromeda*'s cozy galley, by the light of a lantern hanging from the deckhead, the lieutenant collapsed in a dining chair; he was bleeding profusely, on the verge of shock.

"The coat must come off."

"Don't cut it," he said. His voice was weak but the pride was unmistakable.

"Mr. Dalton, will you assist me?"

With Dalton's help I removed his coat, and although the pain nearly cost him his consciousness, Markham made not a sound.

"Now, help me get him onto the table. I'll need one of your men on each limb."

I opened my instrument kit beside him on the table, ignoring the coffee stains and a wood bowl of half-eaten cornmeal mush. Slipped on my surgical apron and then pulled out the scalpel, the tenaculum, the forceps, the needle threaded with catgut. I broke the twine on a stack of pledgets and moved everything into position. I felt strangely calmed, preparing to do my work, purposeful work, in this familiar and practiced manner.

"I'm sorry, but the shirt must be sacrificed." With the scalpel, I laid open the sleeve all the way to the neck. Markham's eyes widened, whether at glimpsing his wound or seeing the flash of sharpened steel held so close to his throat by the man who had shot him, I know not. His left arm, shoulder, and his chest—clammy and white, a fistful of light brown hair in the center, just above his sternum—were exposed now, and his breathing was shallow from pain and shock.

"Dip that bit of rope in some rum, Mr. Dalton, please, sir. It'll give your lieutenant something to bite down on while I examine the damage to his flesh. You'll find a jug of it in the locker beneath the deckboard you're standing on. The mugs are on hooks overhead, just there, next to the lantern."

My instruments ready, within easy reach, the patient prepped, I was ready to begin. The light was dim but, as any good ship surgeon, I was accustomed to working nearly blind. It was as if my fingers developed eyes.

"I'll be as quick as I can, Lieutenant. Tell me, how long have you served the frigate *Richmond*?" I asked to distract him, probing the wound with the tip of my right forefinger, my left hand pushing firmly just below the ridge of the clavicle bone, to coax the ball within reach.

He did not deign to answer, flinching only slightly from the pain. I couldn't help but admire him for that. I probed deeper to find it, and did—lodged neatly in the pocket between the clavicle and the acromion process.

"Hold still now, I've got it... I've got it." His muscles tensed, he drew in a sharp, audible breath as I pried out the lead, a rush of blood flowing warmly across my fingers. I placed the ball on the table, where it rolled slowly to the edge and then along the fiddle, coming to rest beside the bowl of mush.

"A remembrance for you, lieutenant." I could not contain my bitterness, thinking of my friend's body lying on the deck above us, a ball in his brain, his remembrances obliterated. If only I could have helped him.

Dalton stood behind me; I heard his breathing, felt his eyes on me, watching my every move as I further examined the wound and ligated the blood vessel.

"You're a lucky man, Lieutenant Markham. The subclavian vein was torn but I've controlled the bleeding. With the arm immobilized, it should heal nicely, if you give it a few days' rest."

"I didn't know ye were a marksman," Dalton said, dryly. "Ye're a man of many talents; ye should've been a marine."

I remembered that tone of voice well; it was one of the qualities I had loved about him, that edge. I knew it protected a soft heart.

"I have no desire to shoot people—only when they attack my property and kill my men. Besides, the color of the uniform doesn't become me. Hand me those gauze pledgets, if you please, Mr. Gunner." Our hands again touched briefly in the exchange.

"There now, lieutenant, that was the worst of it. You there, marine," I said, looking at the biggest one, whose face was a shade paler than those of his comrades. "Maintain firm pressure here, like this, while I prepare a dressing and immobilizer for your officer."

The man's eyes flew from the wounded lieutenant's face to the gunner's face.

"Do it," said Dalton. Markham nodded, still unable to speak.

I had not enough dressing for a proper bandage, so I tore up my own bed sheet.

"Help him sit up. Slowly, now. On the edge of the table."

Using a long swath in a crisscross fashion, I immobilized his left arm across his chest and draped his bloodied shirt around him, helping him slide his good arm into the remaining sleeve. I then fastened the shirt with a few stitches of catgut. Checking both his radial pulses, I found them to be equal in strength and his hand warm, indicating good blood flow distal to the injury.

"A tot of rum for the patient," I ordered. "Good Rhode Island rum."

Dalton poured him a generous splash and held it to his lips.

"Take it for the pain, lieutenant," I said. "It'll be worse in a few hours; that's to be expected. The packing should be removed and the wound re-dressed in forty-eight hours—sooner if the dressing becomes saturated with blood. In a week you should begin to feel much improved, though I'd advise you not to use your left arm in any capacity for a fortnight."

"I'll have the naval surgeon attend to it," Markham said stiffly, redrawing the invisible boundary between us. "And now we must take you to the frigate, MacPherson. You and your men."

I wiped my hands on my apron, leaving streaks of blood. "You killed my first mate, Lieutenant Markham. Why? Why did you fire upon us? What choice did you give us but to protect ourselves?"

He seemed taken aback by my question, or perhaps it was a grimace of pain that crossed his pale and clammy face. "We are His Majesty's Navy. The marines were under my orders to protect me and to fire if they saw any sign of resistance." He paused to gather his strength. "You should not have evaded us. Mr. Dalton, I give you charge of the shipmaster. Please accompany him to the gunboat and arrange for his confinement aboard *Richmond*. We'll make sail for Providence as soon as it's light and the tide rises, I expect."

Fourteen

Aboard HMS *Richmond*

The frigate loomed and my heart swelled so large I thought it would burst. Up and over the side; it was like coming home and I felt a rush of familiarity envelop me as I stepped onto the deck. For a sweet moment it was as if I had never left. I recalled a hundred little memories, the faces and names of men and a few women who were my brothers and sisters for those months I spent as surgeon's mate. I recalled too, the hundreds of injuries and illnesses I tended to, a constant war my mate Dudley and I fought under ship surgeon Charles Brantigan.

I did not recognize the man who took me in custody, escorting me down the companionway and aft to the gunroom, the cozy wooden cave where I had once spent many hours in good company. My own initials were carved into that smooth oak table, somewhere in that forest of letters.

This frigate—I felt such pride to have been a part of her, such anger and shame when I had been dismissed; yet the shame I felt was undeserved, for I had served her well. One of the midshipmen at the table, looking a little soused, I recognized though he had grown up, had a wisp of a shadow on his chin and above his lip now, and although he looked up with dull interest as I was paraded past, he did not recognize me; he did not remember I had once purged him when he had eaten too much plum pudding, once excused him from duty when he had drunk more than his share of grog, and once brought him soup like a loblolly when he was shivering with a fever. Little Sammy Perkins, who no doubt had come aboard through family interest with some captain or admiral, had been fourteen years old when I served aboard. Now Sammy was Sam or Samuel, a man, though still a midshipman, I guessed.

Ships, like houses, develop their own particular smell. I breathed it in, starved for it, that mixture of damp wood, hemp, tar, bilge water, and bodies in need of a bath—my own adding to the fug. The more I breathed the fainter the odor became, until I could smell it no more; I had become part of it again.

"The captain will question you in the morning, shipmaster," said the man who had escorted me. "Tonight we'll quarter you just here, in the gunner's berth. Consider yourself fortunate to be given such a fine holding cell. There'll be two marines stationed just outside."

Brian Dalton's cabin? My heart squeezed tight like a fist, holding the memory of a certain night long ago. A night that didn't end well.

"And my men?"

"Not to worry, your crew has been pressed into the service of the King. They're proper seamen now," he grinned. "And a crew of our own able seamen sent over to sail the schooner."

The door closed behind me. I sat on Dalton's bed in the blackness—no light had been provided for me. My mind raced, my thoughts chasing themselves. Cyrus was shot dead. Dead! My ship was taken. My former friend was now my enemy. The world was turned upside down.

Fifteen

Aboard *Richmond*
Inside the gunner's cabin

I heard the low murmur of Dalton's voice outside the door as he spoke to the marines. My breath quickened. He knocked, two sharp taps, and then opened the door with a crack and stepped inside, ducking his head to clear the lintel and hanging a lantern on a hook on the deckhead where it cast a cone of warm yellow light. We faced each other, our breath colliding, hot as cannon fire.

"Shipmaster, I have some questions for ye," he said gruffly, and pulled the door shut behind him. Then, rather more softly, "I'm sorry about your mate. I heard no order to fire. I'm afraid one of your men must've fired first."

"The only weapon fired from my vessel was my own—after my first mate fell to the deck. He was cleating off the halyard," I hissed.

"Ye ran from us."

"You had no right to stop us. No right to seize my ship. No right to fire upon us."

"It wasn't my doing. I was only following orders until ye shot my lieutenant. Bloody hell, how was I to know it was ye aboard? And when did ye turn smuggler?"

I fought for my breath, and to keep my voice low. "He's dead. Cyrus is dead. You killed my mate."

"I didn't. And besides, ye evaded a Royal Navy frigate. What the hell did ye expect, Patricia?"

To hear my real name spoken nearly reduced me to tears. "I wrote you," I managed to say. "I asked you to write me, care of the White Horse Tavern. You never did."

"I only received your letter in Norfolk—just last week, in fact. Years late. As unreliable as ye ever were." He slid his hand inside his jacket, under his armpit, and pulled out a folded, wrinkled, water-stained piece of paper, thrusting it at me. "Take it. Please. It's burning a hole in my heart."

I didn't take it, but waited, hoping he would say more. Dalton was a man who took his time forming his thoughts into words.

He crushed it in his hand, choking on emotion. "What in Christ did ye expect me to do, princess?"

The old term of endearment cut through to the heartwood, nearly felling me. So much had happened. I was no longer that impetuous girl he had found belowdecks, full of arrogance and false entitlement.

"What did you expect *me* to do, Brian? I was booted off the ship in New York."

"What do ye mean, what did I expect ye to do? I thought ye were coming with me. I thought we had an understanding. I thought we were to be married and I would be able to keep ye aboard as my wife."

"If you read my letter you know what happened. My services were required. A woman was dying. That young soldier Everett Lee, the man whose leg I amputated—his brother's wife. I went to her aide, and then, I—"

"It was always somebody else, some higher calling. Ye can never know my anguish."

"It seems you've found comfort enough." I held up the woman's shift I had found under the pillow, tossing it at him. He let it fall to the deck at his feet. In the dim lantern light I read everything in his eyes.

He cleared his throat. Stepped closer, inches away. Whispered hoarsely, "It's been three years now. I'm a man, not a monk."

"And I'm a woman, despite my appearance." I thought of Havana and the desire I had felt for the Frenchman—a physical craving, like hunger or thirst.

"Are ye?" His dark eyes widened. "Are ye a woman?"

I could see his carotid pulse pounding, his chest expanding with each breath. I could smell him, a familiar smell I had forgotten until now, filling my head and awakening memories and desire. I stepped forward, pressing myself against his chest—a rough clench of arms, a clash of mouths, more combat than kiss. Outside the door, a low murmur of voices. On the deck above us, footsteps, an order shouted. Never alone on a ship.

I pulled him down on me, onto his narrow bunk, the twisted woolen blanket damp with sea air and sweat. In the darkness our hands, our mouths, our bodies found what they were seeking as we came together at last—not so much a coupling as an act of taking what we needed, of claiming what we had so long desired. All over in a flash—he swallowed my cry with his mouth, my tears wetting our lips.

Afterward, we clung to one another for what seemed a long time, coming to terms with it. The present. There were no whispers of endearments. Our breathing was at odds, my inhale colliding with his exhale. I had gotten what I long wanted but there was no satisfaction in it.

"Who is she?" I said, hearing the petulance in my voice and hating it. Felt him prickle under the questioning. Instantly wished I hadn't mentioned it. Didn't want to know, didn't want to hear her name spoken from his lips, those lips I had just tasted. I had no right to know; I had given up that right.

"Her man drowned. One of our best topmen."

"And you took her in. Of course. How gallant of you. She pleases you."

He rolled off me and sat on the edge of his bunk, not looking at me. "She's a good lass. She's happy to share my cabin. My life. She pleases me, yes. But it's *ye*, woman, I wanted to please."

His words found their mark. I felt their truth. But though I had professed my love to Brian I had not wanted to give up my role as surgeon's mate and the meager hammock space I called my own. I had not wanted to live as the warrants' wives lived, staying out from underfoot, sneaking around like moles belowdecks, playing nursemaid to the young midshipmen and servant boys—and I still didn't—yet I couldn't bear to think of him with another woman. I knew that butter-soft look his eyes took on, that desirous sigh, the hoarse little growl of pleasure deep in his throat. Of course it was inevitable; Brian was the sort of man who couldn't say no to a woman in need—could any man? That was it—she had insinuated herself, she had come knocking on his door needing comfort and wanting to please, and he couldn't refuse her. He was, after all, a man.

Neither of us spoke. The space between us widened like a great river's delta, the Gulf of Mexico, and I was born out to sea on an ebbing tide. So this is how it would end.

He stood and pulled up his breeches, fumbling awkwardly with the buttons. I stood to face him, completely undone.

"Ye look lovely."

"Don't patronize me. I'm hideous," I snapped.

"Come here, love," he whispered. He took me in his arms and kissed me, tenderly this time, cupping his hands over my breasts like they were rare and delicate porcelain tea cups. I felt completely possessed by him. Hated it, loved it, loved him. I would have given myself to him again, but he stepped back.

"I must go. The captain will be down in the morning to interview ye."

"Captain Elphinstone?"

"Nae. It's Captain Collins now. Will ye confess your disguise to him?"

My surrender, my desire, turned to sudden irritation. "What? And destroy my future? Do you not know who I am?"

"But –

"My partners are behind me. Newport is behind me."

"I was behind ye too, once. But that wasn't enough, was it?"

"And what of your girl? This cabin isn't big enough for the three of us."

"As ye wish." His voice was drawn. His face looked suddenly older, creased with worry. "I won't betray ye but I fear ye may lose your schooner. We've been very lucky with seizures and condemnations."

"I'll take my chances."

"We're only doing our duty. What we've been assigned to do. You're the one outside the law."

"And I'm only doing what the merchants of Rhode Island have been doing for generations."

"I don't care about the damned Yankees; I care about you." His face softened, he gripped my shoulders and kissed my forehead. "I'll protect ye if I can. I'll guard your secret, I'll respect your identity if ye wish—but I can nae help ye keep your ship, Patricia."

Sixteen

Aboard *Richmond*

The sound of the ship's bell pulled me up from the depths of a dream, instantly forgotten. Five bells—half past the hour of six. I had dozed off from sheer exhaustion in spite of every intention to remain awake. All around and above me the ship was coming to life, and here I was, waking up in the gunner's bed. Alone.

Someone at the door. *At least they give me the courtesy of a knock.*

I slid hastily from the berth, pulled on my breeches, tucked in my shirt, slipped on my waistcoat and fumbled to button it. Ran a hand across my head, the hair growing out and already beginning to curl.

The door opened. I stood there in my bare feet, shivering. It wasn't the gunner and it wasn't the captain—it was Dudley Freeman, my former shipmate and fellow surgeon's mate. We stared at one another in the dim light and I saw in his big-jawed face a hot stew of emotions.

"It *is* you, the very same. I hadn't believed it when I heard a Patrick MacPherson, shipmaster, had been taken captive. Thought it was a coincidence of name." He stepped inside Dalton's cabin and pulled the door shut behind him. We stood eye to eye, close enough that I could smell the coffee as well as last night's spirits on his breath and from the pores of his skin. He had nicked himself shaving this morning, I couldn't help but notice. Three beads of dried blood on his jutting chin.

"That's uncharacteristic of you, Dudley. To be so careless with your razor," I said.

He touched his face with his fingertips, lightly, quickly locating the minor infliction. Big hands, long digits, dexterous, skillful. I had always admired Dudley Freeman's hands.

"I see you're still presenting yourself falsely," he sneered.

"Clothes make the man," I said in retort, falling into adolescent word-sparring as we had once enjoyed as shipmates together.

"You're such a sham, MacPherson. You've failed as a woman, and as a man."

"But I was a good surgeon's mate. A damned good surgeon's mate and you know it."

"If you were good it's because I taught you to be good. You're ridiculous, that's what you are. And untrustworthy."

"You would have seen me hanged from the yardarm. And all because you were jealous of my affections for someone else."

He licked his long, mule-like teeth. "They used to burn your kind at the stake."

"I'm not accused of witchcraft, Dudley. There's no profit in spells and incantations."

"And there's no profit in smuggling, you're now to discover."

"Is it just me you hate, or all women?"

"What I hate is deceit. You've entered our world twice now under false pretenses, trying to deceive us."

I *had* deceived them; yes, that was true. I had lived among them as a man. I had done a man's work and no one but the gunner had been the wiser. But I had also been one of them. I decided to pursue a different tack.

"So you're ship surgeon now, I presume? Brantigan has surely retired."

"I am indeed. Old Brantigan's blindness and palsy became too extreme to hide. Captain Elphinstone's gone as well; it's a different ship than it was when you strung your hammock beside mine. I'm ship surgeon, but with no war on, there are less interesting cases to operate on. And that brings me to the purpose of my visit. I'm told you dressed our lieutenant's injury—one that you inflicted. Very gentlemanly of you, MacPherson." He leaned against the doorjamb, crossing his arms over his chest.

"Your lieutenant took a bullet to the left shoulder. I removed the ball intact. There was a fair amount of tissue damage and he bled rather profusely, but I predict he'll make a full recovery if the wound is cared for properly. You'll see my work when you examine him. And I think you'll be pleased. I learned much from you, Dudley. You always were excellent with a scalpel, handy with catgut. You taught me the importance of speed and precision. You taught me to put aside my sensibilities and trepidation. You taught me to abolish self-doubt. From watching you I learned once I picked up the scalpel, not to hesitate—it could mean a man's life."

Predictably, he softened at the compliments; I could see it in his face. I really had learned those skills from Dudley Freeman, disagreeable as his nature was.

"And you, MacPherson, are you well? Do you have a wound that needs tending?"

"I'm completely unscathed, thank you. But one of my men was shot dead, and that's what prompted me to fire. I don't suppose, now that you're ship surgeon in full, you've learned how to resurrect?"

His laugh was short and dry. We had both seen so many men die; the death of a stranger meant nothing to him.

"Are we finished? Have you anything else to discuss with me, Dudley? I find myself quite exhausted."

"You'll have plenty of opportunity to catch up on your sleep, I should imagine. Awaiting trial. It was most rash of you to lead us a merry chase, MacPherson. But I'll leave you to your solitude; my day begins."

Outside the cabin door there was a rustling as the marine guards snapped to attention. An exchange of voices followed by the opening of the door. This time it was the captain who came to inform me what I had already suspected: that I was in custody, my ship was impounded, and I was being transported to Providence where my case would be heard by the vice-admiralty court.

Seventeen

December 24
Providence, Rhode Island

Snow was falling, big soft flakes that settled on my eyelashes as I was marched down the street to the courthouse, under marine guard. Fortunately for me, I had a friend in Providence. Everett Lee had seen *Andromeda* sail in just ahead of the *Richmond*. Rowing out to meet me and seeing the prize crew aboard the schooner, he rowed back to alert the men at the wharfs, warehouses, and coffee shops.

The townspeople packed into the courthouse to hear the charges against me and I was glad for their presence. But Judge Andrews was away. The deputy heard the charges and released me on my own recognizance, pending trial. It would not be a jury trial—the vice-admiralty court never tried by jury—and if I wanted legal counsel, I would have to provide my own. I took heart hearing that Judge Andrews was known to be sympathetic to local merchants and shippers.

An hour later I was on the street, a free man until the trial, but a man without a ship or cargo, and confined to the colony. *Andromeda* lay at anchor in the roadstead, under guard; I was not allowed access to collect any of my personal effects still aboard. Among my few possessions was the silver I had been given by the Spanish grandee in gratitude for attending his daughter—I had stowed it under the mattress of my bunk. Surely it had been discovered by now, and either apprehended and impounded—or possibly unreported, stolen by whoever had found it.

The Goddard women, Sarah and her daughter Mary, offered me temporary lodging in their attic bedroom. Mary and Everett quickly composed a special-edition broadsheet announcing *Andromeda*'s seizure, sending it out with errand boys to be sold on the streets and in the taverns and coffeehouses of Providence.

The Goddard home itself was like a private coffeehouse. News and gossip came through the door, borne by clients who came by to deliver and collect letters or to place an advertisement in the *Gazette*. Besides the newspaper, the Goddards printed pamphlets, books, and proclamations. They sold stationery and quills, wrote letters for others, and served as one of Providence's post offices. Because of this, many townspeople found their way to the kitchen table, a sturdy plank table not graced with a cloth on account of printer's ink and coffee stains.

I sat at that table, an hour after my release, drinking West Indian coffee and eating a corn muffin fresh out of the oven, listening to Mrs. Goddard discuss the boycott of British cloth with a local dry goods merchant while Mary greeted customers in the adjoining shop.

In the cellar beneath us Everett was working the press; I could hear the thudding of the ink balls as he pounded the ink, preparing the weekly newspaper. The papers weren't printed on the stamped paper as the new law required—but how much longer would the

Providence *Gazette* be able to flout the tax? Mrs. Goddard had reason to believe a new shipment of stamped papers had arrived on the frigate *Richmond.*

"I assure you there will be trouble in the streets over this," she said. "If the navy attempts to bring the papers ashore, the mob will try to seize them."

We were soon joined at the kitchen table by the Widow Hawthorn, a shipowner who informed me that Dominic Hale's ship had not yet been sighted returning to Newport. His ship was late, but not so late as to cause undue concern. A lot could happen to detain a ship, as I well knew. While the widows talked business, I wrote letters to Dominic's new wife and to our partner, John Eli, explaining the death of Cyrus Lovelace and *Andromeda's* capture, and then letters to our merchants and creditors detailing the loss.

The Widow Goddard presided over her colonial kitchen salon from where she ran her printing business. Fiery letters written by influential men, usually published anonymously, made for popular reading. These letters, along with the shipping news, sold papers, but the business relied heavily on money from private advertisements, public notices, and government proclamations. These paid notices brought in the bulk of the money needed to keep the press running and the Goddard women housed and fed.

Sarah and Mary Goddard had their fingers on the pulse of Providence. News, gossip, opinions—all came through this kitchen and much of it made its way into print in one form or another. Here I had a link to the information Guyon and the Habaneros were so eager for—if only I had my ship.

"The people of Providence stand with Newport. The word is out, and the *Mercury* will follow suit," Mrs. Goddard said, decocting a pot of coffee beans on the stove. The pleasant tinkle of spoons against porcelain cups as we stirred small chunks of brown sugar into the hot black liquid:

"Officially, I may have to discontinue printing when the

stamped paper arrives, for as long as the act is in place. But I assure you I have no intention of ceasing publication altogether. We'll go underground if we have to, until Parliament comes to Its senses. If not repealed—if the act is enforced—it'll be the ruin of us and every other printer in these colonies. Has your trial been set, Mr. MacPherson?"

"As soon as Judge Andrews returns, the date will be set. Meanwhile, my ship and cargo are seized and my men have been pressed into service; I might as well be in prison."

"You are welcome to stay with us until your trial. Our towns are rivals but we all hate the stamp. As for impressment, the navy doesn't discern between Providence men and Newport men, do they? On these issues, we stand together."

As comfortable as the Goddard kitchen was, I couldn't settle in. There was much to be done.

"I must get to Newport today, if possible," I said. "I must personally deliver the news of Cyrus's death to his family, and I must get protection papers for my men aboard *Richmond*."

"Tomorrow is Christmas Day; there likely won't be any traffic between Providence and Newport. Why not accompany the mail on the packet? It leaves at noon, within the hour. And you could take the broadsheets announcing *Andromeda*'s seizure, deliver them to the coffeehouses and taverns—and to the *Mercury*. Sam Hall will certainly want to speak to you about it and write a similar notice for his paper."

Thirty minutes later I was aboard the local mail shallop with eight other passengers, three sacks of mail, and assorted baskets and barrels of oysters, apples, ground corn meal—and a bundle of broadsheets, fresh off the press. As we sailed past my ship I could see two red-jacketed marine guards standing sentry, one at the bow and one at the stern. They looked cold and glum, no doubt thinking they'd rather spend Christmas on land or aboard the frigate *Richmond* rather than their floating outpost.

Eighteen

Newport

Upon landing, I went straightaway to see Mrs. Hale so that she might hear the news from me personally. She received me in her parlor, which was festooned with holly and evergreen garlands and bathed in the light of a dozen candles. From somewhere in the house I heard the voices of children at play. One of them must have been Dominic's daughter. A rush of warmth filled me, to know that Chauncey was here, and well. If only I had something to give her, a bauble or sweetmeat in honor of Christmas. But I had nothing—had not even thought of it until just that minute.

"Do have a seat, captain. I bid you joy on this Christmas Eve."

"I wish I could bid you good cheer, madam," I said, clutching my hat in my hand and remaining on my feet. "Instead, I'm the bearer of bad news, I'm afraid."

Her face, already pale, drained of all color as she sank onto the sofa. "What is it?"

"*Andromeda* has been seized, fully laden, returning to Newport, and my men—our men—are held against their will aboard the frigate *Richmond*."

She breathed deeply and sighed, the color returning to her complexion. "I thought for a moment you had news of my husband's ship."

Andromeda was her husband's ship too, but of course that wasn't what she meant. She was concerned for her husband's life—and the fate of a much larger ship.

"No, madam. I'm sorry if I alarmed you. I've heard nothing of Mr. Hale, but I'm certain he is well. I hope—I'm certain—you'll hear from him soon. But as to our schooner *Andromeda*, there's worse news, I'm afraid."

I had no idea how to soften this next blow, so I plunged on. "Cyrus Lovelace was shot when they boarded us."

"Shot? Cyrus was shot?"

"Yes. Shot defending our vessel. He was by my side." My throat tightened, my eyes blurred.

"Cyrus is dead?"

"Yes, madam. Shot dead at my feet."

She stared at the floor, as if studying it. I heard the children's voices again, ringing out in laughter.

"I understand he was your kinsman," I said. "I am most heartily sorry for your loss."

"Yes, he was my dear cousin's son. He was..." She closed her eyes and drew in a great and shuddering breath.

I went over and sat down next to her, fumbling for my handkerchief and offering it to her. She pressed it to her eyes but made not a sound.

I felt I had failed Cyrus. I felt I had failed Mrs. Hale and Dominic too, in some way. *Andromeda* would have been a small sacrifice to save his life. We shouldn't have run. We should have taken the loss.

"Why? Why did they shoot him?"

"We gave them chase. We kept running even after they fired a warning shot over our bow. Later—after dark—we ran aground entering a salt pond trying to elude them. But they sent an armed boat to apprehend us."

"He died protecting his ship," she said. "They navy has killed one of our boys, a merchant seaman. They should be tried for murder."

"The navy doesn't see it that way."

"If I know Cyrus," she said, "he wouldn't have wanted to hand over the schooner. A passionate young man he was, a scrapper much like his mother, rest her soul. I convinced my late husband to take him on. But who would have guessed he would lose his life for it?" She dabbed roughly at her eyes, her thin red nose, and then crumpled the square of linen in her fist. "The poorer sort, such as Cyrus was, are roused to do rash things in the name of rights, of liberty, yet they seldom stand to benefit from their actions."

"I am sorry."

"I don't blame you, Mr. MacPherson. Captain. You had your orders too. My ships—our ships—we're not accustomed to such treatment. But where this will end, I don't know. I pray Mr. Hale is not assaulted on his return."

"You should know, Mrs. Hale, that I fired back and wounded an officer. It rather complicates things. And there is another matter, a further complication. My men—our men—are being held aboard the frigate against their will, pressed into service. I need their protection papers to have them released."

"You shall have them. As for your share of the cargo, there's nothing I can do. Should Judge Andrews rule against you—and he may, for the Redbones hold no great influence with him—your ship and cargo will be sold at auction. You should know my family has rivals in Providence. They would bid against us, just to drive up the price. My company is stretched thin at the moment and what money and credit we have is invested in Redbone ships. I'm afraid if the schooner is condemned we'll have to cut our losses."

"Sacrifice *Andromeda*, you mean."

Mrs. Hale's eyes were dry now, and clear; her mind, practical and calculating. "I have no choice."

I wondered what Mr. Hale would say to that. And where did that leave me?

Nineteen

**The Lovelace Farm
Rhode Island**

It was nearly dark, a deep blue December twilight, as I set off for the Lovelace farm on a saddle horse rented from the livery stable, courtesy of Mrs. Hale. The blanket of wet snow muffled the ring of hooves against the rocky road and covered fields of flax, hemp, and corn stubble. The farmhouse was built on a rise facing seaward; a glow of lamplight in the windows gave it a warm and cheery look as I approached—a cheer soon to be palled by grief.

Juliana herself answered the door, in a waft of savory smells from the kitchen. She favored her brother so much it startled me. The same fair hair and skin, the same blue-water eyes and wheat-colored lashes. The same full and shapely lips. I wanted to just stare at her face, as if I could conjure her brother back to life.

"I'm Patrick MacPherson, of Hale and Eli Shipping," I said. "Captain of the schooner *Andromeda*. Are you Miss Lovelace?

Juliana Lovelace?"

She must've read the news on my face, or sensed it in some way. A stranger showing up uninvited, unannounced on Christmas Eve. "Come in." She hesitantly opened the door wider.

I stepped into the dark foyer, breathed in the fatty, smoky scents of roasting meat permeating the air. The Christmas meal, being prepared. A servant appeared, a kitchen servant in a stained apron and cap, but Julianna dismissed her with a wave of her hand.

"May I take your hat, captain?"

I removed my tricorn, covered with a dusting of snow, but clutched it to my chest.

"I cannot stay. I don't wish to intrude."

Her eyes locked onto mine, steeling herself for the news. I was aware of a ticking clock nearby at the end of the hallway.

"Something has happened to Cyrus," she said evenly. It was a statement of fact, not a question.

"Is your father at home, Miss Lovelace?"

"He's in town with my brother. I don't expect them home until much later. Would you care to sit down?"

"Yes, perhaps we'd better sit down." I followed her into the simply furnished parlor. She indicated a chair and I sat, but she remained standing.

"You've come with bad news, haven't you, captain? This is not a social call."

"I'd like very much to speak with your father." Some of the snow that had collected on the crown of my hat fell off onto the smooth pine floor.

"But I've told you, my father's not here. It's Cyrus, isn't it? You can tell me, you must tell me. He's been injured, or..."

Our eyes met. She saw the truth.

"He's dead, isn't he?"

My own eyes now stung with unshed tears. I have always been a very forthright person; I could think of no way to put off telling her the truth—the truth which she had already guessed.

"I'm so very sorry, Miss Lovelace. But yes." My voice cracked.

"Cyrus is dead."

Her eyes widened, dry as stones. Her lips tightened; her complexion drained of color. I rose out of the chair and held out my arms, an awkward but sincere gesture. Surprisingly, she accepted my embrace, though she was not ready yet to be comforted; she was still in shock. Perhaps I needed it more than she did.

So this is how I meet your sister, the lovely Juliana. You wanted us to meet, and now we have. I thought then of the kid gloves Cyrus had brought from Havana for her, and how they had been seized by my former mates on the frigate, to be auctioned off to the highest bidder.

"He died honorably," I said, "In defense of the ship. And swiftly. If that matters."

She pulled back now, away from my arms. Even in the dim light I could see her complexion change from pale to paler still—and then growing duskier, darker, livid.

"To Cyrus it might have mattered; he's a man. But what I want to know is how—how did this happen, captain?" She was not so much grieved as insulted; I could see the anger now rising in her face as if she had been slapped. "What happened? Why?"

"Sit down, Miss Lovelace; please let us sit down and I'll tell you how it came about."

I stayed with her until Mr. Lovelace and her brother returned home. The rattle and jingle of harness trappings and wagon wheels, the blowing of horses, alerted us to their arrival; out the window we could see the shadow of the wagon—the wagon that had borne home the body of Cyrus, we were soon to find out. The men bore the pine box into the parlor, to announce the sorrowful news that Julianna already knew. Mr. Lovelace then sent Julianna and her brother from the parlor, and I alone remained with him to hear his torment and his wrath—wrath that was directed at me.

"Are you telling me my Cyrus was shot dead so that a merchant— some rich merchant—my wife's cousin—might avoid her duties?

Her due taxes? And you, you upstart know-nothing pup, running from His Majesty's officers, and for what? To prove a point? To save your employer and your investors a few pounds?"

His eyes were the only thing about him that he had passed on to his eldest son, from what I could see of his stooped, stout frame, his dark hair, his fleshy face. Those bloodshot eyes glowered at me, violet in their rage and pain. "My son, shot and killed, and what for? To avoid paying duties that he did not owe—that he personally was not required to pay? He would have collected his wages regardless. Damn you merchants, you shippers. Damn you Sons of Liberty! To think my boy could've been a farmer. Could've inherited this land, this house. Could've married, had children, and lived to be—" His voice broke but it was not my place to offer comfort to him as I had his daughter; he surely would have hit me. I stood tall, listening to the clock tick, waiting for time to pass.

Mr. Lovelace regained his composure and railed on while I stood, taking it like a man. Looking at the pine box covered with snow, beginning to melt. Hearing his words, feeling his anger, letting his rage run through me, merging with my own. Of course he blamed me. Someone was to blame; someone was always to blame.

Twenty

Newport

Back in Newport I went to see Sam Hall, the publisher of the Newport *Mercury*. I found him not at the print shop but at the tavern next door, hard over in drink. He was in good company; the house was filled with men, all of them quite riotous.

On this Christmas Eve no carols filled the smoky, candlelit room, however, and the talk was not of Bethlehem but of Whitehall. I felt it then, most strongly, coming inside from a cold ride: The anticipation, the fervor, sparking in the air. I heard it then, a collective sense of rebellion, of entitlement, as if we were well-endowed young lords suddenly deprived of our due inheritance. A tavern filled with colonial merchants, shipmakers, and craftsmen—we were all of us demanding our due. I heard it then and I felt it then, too, like a parching thirst or the grip of hunger. The want of self-determination.

I handed the printer a fistful of broadsheets; he stood me a drink.

I managed to corner his attention as the men he was drinking with continued their own heated but somewhat disjointed discussion.

"The Widow Goddard sends these, along with her regards."

"And the lovely Miss Goddard?" His bloodshot eyes twinkled.

"I couldn't say, sir. Too occupied with my own problems, as you can see."

He glanced at the broadsheet detailing my arrest. "Bloody bastards. I'll write a notice for the *Mercury*. When is your hearing?"

"When the judge returns."

"Judge Andrews?"

"So I'm told."

The publisher nodded his approval. "His sympathy toward us is well known. Any word from Hale?"

"None, sir. Perhaps he's had some intelligence and is delaying his return to a more favorable time. Have you any correspondence for Providence?"

"Yes. Send the Goddard women my very best regards. And tell Sarah my offer still stands."

"Which one are you angling for?" I ventured. "Mother? Or daughter?"

"Either. Both!" He laughed humorlessly, raised his glass, draining the last drops. "What I really want is their printing press. The Goddard business and all its assets." He squinted at me, and winked conspiratorially. "But the women are fair enough, though temperamental." Then covering a belch, he called for the server to tally his account.

"Say, MacPherson, shall we go a-rambling? I know a snug little house where the girls are very warm and welcoming—and lonely, no doubt, on this night before Christmas. No family have they, to have a cup of wassail with. What say we go spread some cheer amongst them?"

I started to protest, for fear of being found out, but then thought better of it. From what I had heard, there was no better place to gather news and gossip than a brothel. Perhaps I would learn something that would be of interest to my contacts in Havana—or something pertinent to my own case, a much more pressing matter. How I would manage spending time with a doxy without revealing myself, I wasn't yet sure, but being a woman, I felt I could manipulate a woman. If I failed at that I might at least buy her confidence and develop an alliance that might have future value for me. Knowing what I did of men and their desires, I wagered many things went on behind the boudoir door, and sometimes, surely, nothing much at all. Knowing what I did of women and their motivations gave me reason to believe I could pull this off. Besides, I was in sore need of a place to lay my head until morning.

Hall settled his account with the tavern keeper's wife. His companions were deep into their cups and no longer coherent. He rose, somewhat unsteadily, and made his way to the door, fumbling to button his overcoat against the cold night. I followed, emboldened by my one drink—and the knowledge that I had little left to lose in this world. If a trollop found me out, so be it.

Twenty-One

The Brothel

Madam Betsy's house was well known in Newport, though it looked quite unremarkable, neither better nor worse than the tavern on one side of it and the hat maker on the other. Men hear of these houses; they know where to find them. They're in every port I've ever sailed into, yet I had never stepped foot inside one.

Four hats and greatcoats hung on hooks along the hallway, bespeaking the presence of other patrons. Who spends Christmas Eve in a bawdy house? Men far from home. Men without families. Men like me.

"Sam! How have you been, my dear? Very busy, I suppose. Oh, but we've missed you so."

Madam Betsy greeted us in a waft of French perfume, clad in

a silk banyan and slippers, her hair spilling down her shoulders in artful disarray. She was no longer young—there were creases around her painted mouth and a cushion of fat beneath her skin—but she was a handsome woman. She was successful. She was a woman in her prime.

"You've brought a friend, I see. Come, sit down, gentlemen. Let me get you some refreshment. Rum punch, sirs? Madeira? Brandy?"

"Brandy," said the publisher, rubbing his hands to warm them.

"I'll have the same," I said, following his lead.

We sat in the parlor, which seemed to serve as the business office as well; it was small and not well heated, but lavishly appointed. Red velvet drapes were drawn across the window to discourage drafts and prying eyes. Overstuffed chairs; a sagging French *canapé*, its fabric worn to a sheen; and on the wall above Madam's desk, a *fête champêtre* painted in the French style. A *femme d'affaires*, Madam Betsy. A woman of business. And I, a man in the market for intelligence, not sexual encounters.

"Do have a seat, gentlemen. Hespera will bring your brandy and nuts. Sam, is it Athena you're wanting to spend time with tonight?" She gave him a playful smile. "That girl has been pining away for you."

Hall grinned. "I do, yes ma'am, and for the rest of the night."

"Of course, Sam; I'll have Hespera take you upstairs after she brings your refreshment."

"And you, sir," she said, extending me her well-manicured hand, which I clasped clumsily in my calloused one. "Shall we discuss your tastes? What is it you desire tonight?"

As Newport's printer stumbled up the steps after the servant in petticoats, I watched as Madam Betsy opened an accounting ledger and then, very businesslike, picked up a quill and dipped it in the inkwell.

"By what name shall we call you, sir?"

I hesitated, wondering if I should give a false name, a pseudonym. But Sam hadn't.

"Patrick," I said, a bit too breathlessly. I cleared my throat for courage.

"First time, Patrick?" she asked, glancing at me kindly.

"No, ma'am," I said. Which was true. "I'm a widower, ma'am." Which was almost true. I was a widow.

"Ah, so young to be wed, much less widowed. But you're not accustomed to this sort of entertainment, are you?"

I nodded. True enough.

"Well then, what sort of experience are you looking for tonight?" She looked at me with the keen and practiced eye of a tailor, sizing me up. "We have girls to suit every purse and every desire. We have the young and we have the boyish, the fat and the lean. We have the motherly who will hold you in their arms and kiss your face, or punish you, if you've been wicked. We have the naughty girls who will do anything you wish, and expertly, without a question asked. We have the submissive, the domineering. We have the pale-skinned and dusky-hued. Perhaps you wish for some companionship, and only that? Tell me, Patrick, what's your pleasure?"

When I didn't answer immediately, she turned back to her books, writing something carefully in the margin, then blowing on it to dry the ink. "We're very discreet. We keep our clients' names and affairs confidential. What sort of girl would you like to spend an hour with? Or the evening?"

I wanted information, not pleasure. But I didn't wish to reveal my intent to the madam—at least, not yet. I had no idea where her interest and her loyalties lay.

"My ship has been seized—my ship and all its cargo. I can't pay you tonight, but I can pay you and I will pay you, you have my word."

She waved her hand dismissively. "You're with Sam; Sam's word is good; he's spoken for you. I'm happy to extend you credit, sir. Besides—I never forget a face." No doubt she had ways of collecting.

"Thank you, ma'am."

"No need to be anxious. You'll find my girls amiable. Very understanding. Most desirable. I would recommend for you Persephone, Lyra, or Eos."

"I want a girl who knows the needs of mariners," I said, feeling my face grow hot. "A disciplined lass. One who has—who knows— the needs of naval officers."

Madam Betsy was completely unruffled. "Eos, she's a salty one. She knows how to obey orders—or give them, if that's your preference. In fact, you're fortunate; she's available tonight. Yes, Eos, she's your girl. Though she comes at an officer's price."

"How much will it cost me?"

"I'll give you the local rate, on credit, as I said. Payable at the end of the month. Two shillings an hour—or a crown for the whole night, from now until eight bells tomorrow morning. There's a ship's clock in her room." She smiled, revealing a good set of teeth. "Rings the half hour, just like you naval men are accustomed to."

Eos answered the door in her chemise and bare feet, her dark hair in tumbled disarray over her shoulders. Inside her chamber the woodstove gave off a toasty warmth. "Don't say a word to the madam, cos I've just about used my week's allowance of firewood," she implored conspiratorially. "I've not had the pleasure, sir. Of entertaining you before. Is it the frigate you serve? His Majesty's *Richmond*?"

"That depends."

Her quick, dimpled smile and a flash of white teeth revealed her youth; I judged she was not above eighteen or nineteen years of age, and in relatively good health.

"Depends on what?"

"On whether or not you've had a bad experience with Richmonds," I bantered, feeling quite nervous all of a sudden. I looked around the Yankee boudoir, a practical and sparely furnished room, but for the lavishness of the woodstove and the Gobelin tapestry hung over the window. A ship's clock sat on the chest of drawers, just as Madam Betsy had said. "Will you please snuff the candles?"

"Let me guess, you're new at this." She pulled her chemise over her head, tossing it on the foot of the bed, and stood naked for me to examine, unabashed as a fishwife displaying her catch. I drew in a sharp breath at the sight of her body, well formed, if thin. Clavicles prominent, breasts like two upturned teacups. Long slender legs, a gap at the crotch. Except for her breasts, fuller than mine, I might have been looking at my own self in the mirror. She held out her hands, whiter and smoother than mine. I pulled her close to me and pressed my lips against her forehead, then impulsively kissed her thin lips, noticing the slight metallic taste.

"Listen, Eos, I'm not new at love and I'm not here for love. Though you are very lovely indeed." And she was, at least in the dim light. Perhaps I was, too—lovelier than I thought. My late husband had thought me so.

"Not for love? Then what are you here for?" She dropped my hands and stepped back.

"To talk. Just to hear a woman speak."

She sighed, thinking she understood. "Oh, you're one of them. Well, you wouldn't be my first." She sighed again as she climbed into bed, completely at ease with her nakedness. "Well, that suits me. I'm a good listener."

"No, I don't have much to say, really. What I want is to hear your voice. Tell me what it's like here. What your days and nights are like."

"You want to hear *me* talk? You want to hear about what I do with other men, perhaps? Some men do." She patted the bed next to her. "Come to bed, then, sir." She smiled and blew out the candles.

I took off my waistcoat and stock, folding them carefully and placing them on the chest of drawers. Pulled off my shoes and lined them up under the bed, the way I had been taught in school. Aware of her eyes on me, I fumbled to unbutton my breeches and stepped out of them, rather awkwardly hopping on one leg, reaching for the poster on the bed for balance. Peeled off my stockings, glad my feet were not too odorous. Now all I had on was my shirt, and that was staying on. I climbed into the bed and lay down next to her, pulling the quilt up to my chin like an old married woman.

We lay there a moment, side by side, saying nothing. A log in the stove snapped and popped. "What shall I call you, sir? You can give me an alias, if you want. Or I can give you a name. Rex or Charleton? I can call you Captain, if you like. Or Admiral," she teased.

"Patrick. Call me Patrick. But tell me about yourself, Eos. It burdens me to talk. I want to listen to you talk, the way some women prattle on, emptying their heads without thinking."

"Well, Patrick, there ain't much to tell. I came to Newport on a British warship; I'm used to the needs of the quarterdeck. They ain't a bad lot. No better, no worse than other men. But they generally don't leave much in the way of gratuities so I don't go out of my way to please them. It depends if their latest prize was prosecuted—then they tend to be more generous. Lately, it hasn't gone well for them, especially here in Rhode Island. Halifax, that's the place for a sure verdict." She snorted into her pillow. "But you're an officer yourself, ain't you? You speak like one."

"I was once a surgeon's mate. But these days I'm a merchantman."

"We have that in common then, you and me. We both quit the navy." A little laugh, more of a girlish giggle, and wiggled her bare feet under the covers. "If I didn't know better, I'd say we have even more in common."

"What do you mean?"

Something about the darkness, and the intimacy of the bedroom, made such a conversation possible. "No insult intended, but if I didn't know better, I'd say you weren't a man, but a woman." Her inquisitive hand found its way to my thigh.

"Why? Because I'd rather talk to you than take advantage of you?"

"It's more than that. I get some customers that only come for the pretense. Men with unnatural desires. But they're still men." Lightly and ever so slowly, she moved her fingers higher, to the hem of my shirt. I froze.

"Must a man disrobe to prove himself a man to you?"

"It ain't that, though most of them do. They can't help themselves; they have this great, urgent need to take or be taken. But I have a sensitive nose, you see. And men and women don't smell the same."

I tried to calm myself, to slow down my breathing, to still my heart. "Are you suggesting I smell like a woman?"

She took her time answering and the silence rang loud in my ears. Her hand rested on my hipbone, fingers tapping lightly.

"It's no business of mine what you are," she said at last, and rather gently. "But you've hired me to talk, and you've asked me to be honest. Have you gotten your money's worth?"

My turn to laugh. "I like you, Eos. I hope we can talk again, and soon."

"I assure you, I'm better at talking with my hands, sir. And my tongue." A little laugh.

A thrill ran through me but I let it go. "Keep your ears open for me. I want to know the comings and goings of the navy ships and whatever you can learn from the officers."

"Oh, I'm to be a spy, then? For the Sons of Liberty? I rather fancy that."

"Not a spy, exactly. Spying is dangerous. Spying can get you hanged. You are to be my confidant. Just stay alert for information. Be a good listener and remember what they say. You can write me in care of Mrs. Goddard, of Providence."

"Well, generally they don't say much, except to tell me what pleases them. Sometimes they're too drunk to say much or do much."

"Flatter them, then. Draw them out. You know how to do it. And when I come to see you, I'll pay you for this gossip." Though how I would manage to pay her was yet to be determined.

"I could post you a letter. I can write tolerably well. What I can't spell I can draw. I'm quite good at figures; I have a knack for sketching. I used to draw likenesses for the officers. But lying with them pays better."

I smiled.

"Would you like to see one of my drawings? In the morning I'll show you."

"How do you afford the paper?"

"I can't." A little snort of satisfaction. "But I've an eye for collecting scraps. Sketching over top of old broadsheets and pieces of old wallpaper."

"Any news you can provide me with, I can use."

Her little snuffling laugh in my ear. "But how will you know I'm not making it up? Feeding you false information?"

"I suppose I won't know. Not right away. But I'll pay you whether you give me any useful news or not."

She seemed to think about this. Then, "Why would you do that, sir?"

"Because I think you're worth it. I'm willing to take that chance." In reality, I had no idea why I would do that. I was out on a limb, I was playacting, but then so was she. Her name was not Eos, I wagered. "I'll pay you for your drawings."

"Hmmm," she murmured, snuggling closer, and I captured her playful hand as it drifted toward my sex again.

"Let us be friends. Just friends."

She wiggled her fingers, interlacing them with mine, and squeezed back. "Friends? I ain't sure I've ever had one, nor if I know what's required. But an informant, that seems straightforward enough."

We lay in silence for a few minutes listening to the ticking clock and the winter wind in the eaves. I realized it didn't matter if Eos suspected I was female, or even if she discovered the fact. We were neither of us who we pretended to be.

"Patrick, there is one thing I've noticed you might be interested in. The *Cygnet* has been in port for some months and recently the frigate *Richmond* has come in and out. But the officers haven't been in to visit us very much. They've not been well."

"Not well? Are they poxed?"

"No, it's fever and the hacking cough they suffer from. I took ill myself and missed two nights, a few weeks ago. Felt like bloody hell—aching bones, burning up in bed, coughing up the phlegm, thought I was dying. Madam says it's to be expected this time of year." She withdrew her hand from mine and coyly played with the short curls of hair behind my ear. "I don't suppose that's the kind of information you want to hear, but that's all I know. Except to say that when they're healthy the navy men are randy good lovers." Her laugh was a soft snort against my neck. She found my hand again and I welcomed it.

Within minutes she was asleep, her lips parted slightly, our fingers still entwined. I lay awake a long time, listening to the sound of her breath and mine, like waves lapping the shore. I was certain I couldn't sleep, my mind and heart were racing so—not because of the warm female body next to me, but worry for my ship, my men, and my own future.

A full bladder woke me; it was quarter past four, by the ship's clock on the mantle. Except for the clock's measured ticking, everything was silent. Eos slept on, curled up like a question mark, facing away from me, a tumble of hair obscuring her face. Damp, cold, the windowpane thick with frost, and beyond it, the bleak darkness of a Rhode Island winter morning. Christmas morning.

I stoked the fire and added the last log to warm the room for her, sparks snapping as hungry little flames jumped to life out of the ashes. Buttoned my waistcoat with cold fingers, slipped into my coat, donned my wig and hat. Then, leaving my last shilling on her dresser top as a gratuity, I slipped out of the room and down the narrow creaking stairs, grabbed my hat and coat off the hook, and opened the door. A tabby cat, huddled outside next to the frozen-over rain barrel, saw her chance and slipped inside as I left.

I took the only boat available on Christmas Day—a coastal trader going back home to Providence with a delivery of oysters, ale, apples, and the mail.

Twenty-Two

Aboard *Richmond*

"It's unlawful," John Eli said, red-faced with anger. "You cannot press our men; you have not that right. Here—their papers—you'll find them all in order. The court will stand behind them, and you know it."

Collins didn't even look at the documents that lay before him on the captain's table—a table stained with rings and cluttered with an assortment of empty wine bottles. Instead, he motioned for his clerk, a hunched and bespectacled man in a frazzled wig, to examine them as he reached for his pewter mug, still steaming. The great cabin smelled of last night's brandy and plum pudding. A drizzle of hard sauce glistened on the table in front of me.

Richmond's former commander had been so much more worthy of his commission. Captain Elphinstone, the man who had thrown me off the ship in New York, had at least earned my grudging respect for his position. I wondered what had become of Elphinstone—and why this man now sat in his cabin. Likely Elphinstone had retired. Was sick or injured. Perhaps he had died.

"A fine thing for a couple of smugglers telling me what is lawful after you evaded me and wounded my lieutenant. You're fortunate that I allowed you on my ship and gave you audience."

The clerk squinted to read the papers, which made a little rubbing noise in his gnarled, tremulous hands. He then handed them to the captain. "Indeed, sir; the two Blacks are property of the Redbone family enterprise. The white man is apparently a Rhode Island native, born and bred, in the employ of the same."

Collins gave the papers a glance and then looked at us, his stern gaze going from my eyes to Eli's, and back again to mine.

"Just as I expected. Mr. MacPherson, Mr. Eli, know this: I'm not pressing your Blacks into service—I'm seizing them as property. Everything aboard the schooner has been impounded, pending trial by the authority vested in me. Your other man, the white man, will be released when convenient. Now then, you are interrupting our Christmas observance. I'll see you in admiralty court."

"Where are they? I'd like to see them," I said. "Our Rhode Island men."

Captain Collins rose to his feet, his stubbled face reddening. "That's quite impossible; my men are busy."

"I demand to see them," I persisted, most unreasonably. I felt Eli flinch, knew I shouldn't have said it.

"You don't demand anything aboard my ship," Collins snapped. "You have no rights here, you're nothing but a brigand, you're lucky you're not locked up in a cell. My patience is worn out. This meeting is at an end." He looked to the marine standing at the door. "Sergeant, escort these men to their boat."

On the way out I looked for Dalton or Freeman, anyone I knew from before, but did not see a familiar face. What I noticed was a paucity of men, both sailors and marines. Was the frigate that undermanned? Were they sick, as Eos suggested? Or was it simply a lay day, the Christmas holiday, that made *Richmond* seem so deserted?

Twenty-Three

Providence

"I say we steal it back," I said quietly, leaning over the table to make myself heard to my companions over the din of the crowd.

John Eli, Everett, and I were supping in company with the Goddard women at the Ram's Head, smoky and boisterous that evening with revelers and wassailers enjoying what stood for a Rhode Island tavern feast: stewed mutton bone broth, roasted wild goose, and apples baked in cornmeal, all washed down with ale and spiced rum punch.

Everett's eyes brightened at the notion. "Take back what's been stolen from you. Yes, brilliant idea, Patrick. Count me in."

"Hold on a minute," said John, who, with wife, baby, and farm to consider, was more cautious. "Let's not go off half-cocked. It may be more prudent for us to bear the loss if Judge Andrews rules against us. Which he may. He's pressured by our illustrious collector of customs and his band."

"Why take a chance?" Everett countered. "Judge Andrews can't condemn the ship if there isn't a ship to condemn. We all know that, we've seen it. It happened not long ago in Baltimore. And it's been done here."

We paused our conversation as the innkeeper's wife approached, face flushed, her cap askew, hair astray, foaming pitchers of ale in each hand.

John raised his index finger. "On my account, Mrs. Bevins, please."

"God bless you, sirs and ladies, this one is on the house. Happy Christmas."

"Hear, hear. And to you and Mr. Bevins." We all raised our glasses. The matron left one of the pitchers and hurried off to deliver the remaining one.

John busied himself refilling our glasses until she was out of hearing range. Then, in a low voice, "How do you propose to do it?"

"The *Richmond* is undermanned," I said. "Apparently the press hasn't been very successful. I'll wager *Andromeda* isn't heavily guarded."

Eli nodded. "Some sort of disturbance to draw their attention."

"The stamps," Sarah said. "The stamped papers haven't been brought ashore yet. When they are, they'll be heavily guarded, I should think. It would help to know when they'll be brought ashore— and where they're to be taken. The customs house, I assume. Or perhaps the courthouse. In the early hours, I suspect."

"If we were to provoke a disturbance then," Mary suggested.

"Call up a crowd and follow them," Sarah said, picking up on her daughter's thought. "Enough of a threat so that more marines are sent ashore."

"We could light up another straw man. Flames always draw a crowd." This from Everett, surprising no one.

"We'd have to find out how many men are stationed aboard *Andromeda*," I said. "The wind would have to be favorable."

Eli chewed his cheek in contemplation. "At night, if there's no fog, I can sail us back to the cove near my wharf. I can set lookouts on the shore with lanterns to guide us. *If* we were to do it," he added. "Which I don't recommend. Understand that."

But I knew from the look of concentration and the new light in his eye that my partner was already onboard; the ship was ours.

But how to actually get back aboard *Andromeda*? And once aboard, then what? Was I prepared to kill someone if I had to?

After walking back to the Goddards' house—the snow hard-packed and frozen, Everett's wooden leg slipping, Mary reaching out to steady him, his pride-hurt curse splitting the frigid night air—I lay awake in my bed in the cold, damp garret, huddled under a homespun blanket until first light brightened the windowpane. I was thinking of Brian Dalton. I had to see him again.

Twenty-Four

Providence
The Kings Arms Tavern

I spent much of the day walking the wharf in sight of *Richmond*, hoping to see him. There was little activity on the frigate until late afternoon when a jolly boat of blue jackets made their way to shore. Brian wasn't among them, nor was anyone else I recognized. I followed them into the King's Arms Tavern, where officers and warrants from the warships were said to drink.

Inside, it was nearly empty but for a few old men.

I went up to the bar, hoping for some information.

"New in town, ain't you, sir?" the innkeeper greeted me. "Are you with the frigate?"

"No, sir." I felt a pang of remorse as I said that. A part of me would always be with that ship. "I'm from Newport."

"I won't hold that against you. Will you be needing a room for the night?"

"No. I'm waiting for the *Richmond's* gunner. Mr. Dalton. Are you acquainted with him?"

The innkeeper shook his head. "I don't bother to learn their names. I just take their money and serve them their swill. They'll be drinking hearty for a few nights, I suspect. Celebrating their prize, that local schooner anchored out there in the roadstead."

Painful, hearing the fact so nonchalantly stated from a stranger's lips.

"That's my ship," I said. "*Andromeda.* She's out of Newport—Hale and Eli Shipping. I'm Patrick MacPherson, shipmaster and captain."

"William Nichols, proprietor." A flicker of sympathy crossed his face. "I'm sorry for your troubles. What are you drinking captain.?"

"I'd like a pint of ale, thank you. While I wait. And something to eat, if you please."

He brought me my ale and a bowl of chowder.

Nichols leaned his head over, close to my face. "I thought you should know, captain, I heard someone say last night they plan to sail the prize to Halifax. Where they know they'll get a conviction."

"They can't do that. The deputy has already arraigned me. The trial is to be here in Rhode Island by the vice-admiralty judge."

"The navy has your ship. Who's to stop them? But you didn't hear that from me, sir. These men are my good customers."

"Then why did you tell me, Mr. Nichols?"

He leaned closer. "I don't believe our navy should be pitted against the people it serves. Nor do I believe our navy should press our local watermen to do their revenuer's work."

I raised my glass in agreement.

"None of our own boys come here to drink if there's a warship up this end of the bay," he said. "Afraid they'll be taken. I've raised my prices to compensate for the loss of business." His lip twitched in what sufficed for a wry grin. "Just a little surcharge. In fact, they're buying your beer tonight. They don't know it, but they are."

A group of four men, navy by their swagger, came through the door—but Brian Dalton was not among them. Nichols left me to wait on them. No one approached me; I was an outsider, invisible. I drank my pint and had another, maybe two more, listening for his voice, watching for him to walk through the door. He never did. When I left, the air in the inn was thick and warm with pipe smoke and conversation; in the corner by the hearth a fiddler rosined his bow and drew it across the strings, the sound reaching inside me as if it were my tendon strings that bow caressed.

Outside, I elbowed my way through a crowd that had gathered, men shouting drunken oaths, women's harping stridently. I was trying to make my way back to my attic bed at the Goddards, uncertain of the way, my head swimming with ale. There was some sort of altercation, a disturbance. A boat was missing. I wanted to get away unseen, but someone bumped into me, another grabbed at my arm.

"You there, who are you with?" The man's breath was fired with rum. "State your business."

"Let me pass," I said, slurring in spite of myself. "I'm no part of this."

"Where's our boat?"

"Take your hands off!" I pulled free but someone grabbed my arms from behind, pinning me. Trapped, I roared, a beastly sound, and kicked out like a mule against the injustice. A curse and a moan; a figure dropped to his knees on the cobblestones. I thrashed, I swore, but my arms were still pinned behind me. I was helpless to escape.

Then came a blinding pain in my head—oblivion.

Twenty-Five

Narragansett Bay

I awoke in the bottom of a boat, my throbbing head resting on a coil of line. I gingerly touched my face. So thick, and senseless as a wooden carrick head. Was this my face? A sharp, searing pain through my left jaw convinced me it was. Then I discovered my nose—horribly swollen—a sow's nose. Oozing blood. I struggled to get up, my head pounding against the effort.

"Easy there, captain."

I saw his legs, his shoes, on either side of me. Brian, in the sternsheets, rowing. Looking down at me.

"What? Where?"

"You're with me in a boat. I pulled you out of a street brawl. You really should watch who you associate with, MacPherson."

I groaned and eased myself back down. No, that was worse. "Oh, damn it all—help me up, would you?"

His hand found mine and pulled me to a sitting position. I

leaned against his knee, struggling to stay conscious.

"Breathe deep, it'll clear your head. Here's my handkerchief."

I dabbed at my nose, flinched at the pain. "Where are you taking me?"

"Away from that lot."

"Are you taking me prisoner?" I sat up slowly, between his legs; felt the heat of them. My head throbbed, my face hurt.

"Nae. To safety."

The wind came up, bitter with freezing rain. Brian shipped the oars, laying them in the bottom of the boat next to me, and then raised sail and set off across the bay.

"I don't understand. How is that possible?"

"They're after ye, Patricia. *We're* after ye. The captain means to apprehend ye."

"But I've been released, pending trial." My brain was foggy, but I clearly remembered being released at the courthouse.

"All that's changed now." Brian's voice was tight and strained.

"How?"

"Lieutenant Markham is dead."

"Dead?" I felt suddenly ill, tasted blood in my throat, fought the urge to vomit.

"He died last night. Suddenly." Brian adjusted the tiller and eased the sheets, changing course slightly. "Freeman is blaming you. Because of the gunshot wound. Freeman's saying you killed the lieutenant."

My God, have I killed him? I began to shake, suddenly terribly cold. Brian gave me his coat, wrapping it around my shoulders, but it did no good. The chill I felt was from within.

"Another man, a young private, one of the marines—he died this morning as well."

"What? Was he shot too?"

"Nae. A sickness is going through the ship. A cold, an ague of some sort. A lot of us have been ill with fever and cough. Mr. Freeman has been bleeding and dosing the men. Sending them back to duty as soon as they can stand. He bled Markham—just before he died."

"Do you think he died of the fever? Or from the wound?"

"Doesn't matter what I think. I'm not the ship surgeon, nor am I the captain."

I began to shiver uncontrollably. Brian's coat was warm enough but the chill was from within.

"How did you find me?"

"Luck, mostly. I'm on liberty tonight; I have use of a boat. I had to find ye before anyone else."

I hugged his legs, one on either side of me. Whispered my thanks.

"They mean to take ye and your schooner to Halifax for trial." His voice cracked. "Ye could hang for this, Patricia."

"Where are you taking me? Not to *Richmond*. Am I under arrest?"

"Nae. Not to *Richmond*. And you're not under arrest—I'm bloody rescuing you, or trying to."

"Are we going to *Andromeda*?"

"Nae, are ye mad?"

"Then where? Where are you taking me?"

"To safety. There's a shed. Just down the bay."

"You're taking me to a shed?"

"A boathouse or fisherman's shelter. Seems to be abandoned. We'll have a look at your face."

Brian turned the boat shoreward; we grounded on a stony beach. He leapt out and pulled us to the water's edge, holding out his hand to steady me. I followed him a short distance to a wooden building. He pushed open the door and I followed him inside, out of the wind and icy rain. I breathed in the odor of tidewater muck and fish long dead.

Brian lit a lantern he had brought from the boat, filling the enclosure with warm yellow light. A single room, perhaps ten feet by twelve. There were a few barrels and coils of hemp along the far wall. A pile of oyster shells and an empty bushel basket in the middle of the dirt floor. Beside it, a tar-stained hessian sack.

"The captain's impounded your sea chest, all of your belongings. But I brought ye what supplies I could scrounge—in case ye have to hide out here awhile—along with one of my own shirts and a pair of wool socks." He hung the lantern on a nail on the rafter overhead and retrieved a blanket from on top of one of the barrels, spreading it on the ground. "Sit ye down, let me have a better look at that face."

Feeling a rush of gratitude, I did as he bid, tilting my swollen face up toward the yellow lantern light, feeling ugly and vulnerable.

"My nose," I said, my voice sounding like I had a bad cold. "It hurts."

"Of course it hurts; it's likely broken. It'll hurt worse tomorrow. Ye should know that, having been a surgeon's mate."

"Don't scold me. I've never suffered a broken nose before."

"Well, I have. And I'm not scolding ye, damn it, I'm trying to help ye. Open your mouth, let me have a look at your teeth."

I did as he said, feeling my swollen tongue, my aching jaw. With his blunt forefinger, Brian pressed gently on each tooth in turn. The taste of tar and tobacco mingled with the taste of my own blood.

"Good solid teeth, and all there, as far as I can tell. Your tongue's a might ragged; it must've got in the way."

He pulled out a flask from his pocket. "Here, rinse your mouth."

I was glad to, and glad for the burn of the rum on my gums and tongue. Spat it out onto the dirt floor.

"Hold still, let me see your face." He felt the bridge of my nose between his thumb and forefinger. "Does that hurt?"

"Of course it hurts, my entire face feels like a bruised plum. God, I must look a fright."

"Ye're going to look worse tomorrow, I promise you."

He took off his neckerchief, wet it with the rum, dabbed at the blood on my cheeks and my swollen upper lip. Then without warning he kissed me, barely touching my bruised lips with his. I breathed in his warm exhalation, and although my face still hurt, I didn't mind it so much when his hands caressed my neck, cradling my head as he lay me down on the blanket where he tenderly undressed me, the air cold against my flesh but hot where his fingers and lips touched me. He loved me slowly, exquisitely, as if we had all night, as if we had forever, and I loved him as best I could, almost forgetting about my hurting head, my ravaged face. When I cried out it was not from the pain of my face but a mixture of ecstasy and anguish, of having him and knowing I was losing him forever.

We lay in a tangled heap, my head resting on his arm, his breath in my ear, our clothes strewn haphazardly about, one edge of the blanket pulled over us. I dared not say it, ask it, though it was on my mind, but tried to accept the pleasure and contentment I felt throughout my body—a satisfaction I knew was only temporary. Everything is temporary; nothing lasts.

When we woke it was still dark, but I knew it was morning. I felt the damp cold stealing in and moved closer to Brian, pulling the rough woolen blanket up around our ears, feeling him grow hard against my thigh. A sudden rush of heat and we made love again and when it was over he wiped the blood that dripped from my nose with his hand then helped me dress before dressing himself.

"Are ye well?"

This was it; he was leaving. "I'll be all right. And you?"

"I must get back to the ship."

"Must you?" I found my shoes, cold and stiff.

He helped me to my feet. "Ye know I must. It'll be light soon."

"You could stay here," I said, hearing the desperation in my voice. "With me."

"And help ye steal your schooner back?" He shook his head. "Nae, Patricia. I have a ship, ye know that. And a duty. I'm nae a smuggler."

"The girl. That woman. You love her." It was not a question but an accusation.

He shook out the blanket we had slept on and folded it, but said nothing. Still I pressed him; I had to know.

"Your silence on the matter affirms it."

"She's pregnant, Patricia."

Of course she was; it was the way of things. "How nice. You must be so happy. Is it yours?"

My voice was bitter, yet he had done no crime. Nor had he betrayed me. And now he was putting himself at great risk to help me escape.

He looked at me, caught my eyes with his, and I could not bear it but neither could I look away. "Yes. Mine. It might have been ours."

The tears came, unbidden and unstoppable. I allowed him to hold me, pressing the side of my swollen face against his chest, feeling the pounding of his heart, the movement of his ribcage.

"I don't know how to protect ye now. If ye were my wife, I would know what to do. If ye were an ordinary woman, I'd know how to help ye. Is there anyone you trust in these parts who will take you in? Some place ye can hide out until we sail for Halifax?"

"You know I won't stand for it."

He shook his head. "Damn ye, woman. Do ye want to get yourself killed?"

"I want my ship. What I've worked for. I have nothing else."

"I can nae can help ye in this madness."

"I know that."

He pulled me to him, cupping my swollen face in his hands. "I don't want ye to do it, but if it's to be done, it must be done quickly. Tonight. Send some of your Rogue Island scoundrels to do the deed for ye, if ye must do it. Tonight, after the watch is set, there will only be four men aboard the schooner until morning. Three marines, one able seaman. Two of them are just out of sick berth, though they must not be underestimated."

"What of my crew? Your captain has no right to press them."

"We need men, at least to get to Halifax. Besides, maybe your Africans would prefer freedom. Working an honest living."

"A seaman on a British warship is hardly a free man. They have a good life in Rhode Island."

"Says ye. They might disagree. I know I'd rather be a free man serving a frigate than a slave for a pack of Yankee smugglers."

"It isn't smuggling, what we do; it's how things have been done here for a hundred years."

"So it's 'we' now, is it? It's what 'we' do? So quick to call yourself one of them." He snorted. "Look, I know what you're planning. Just promise me ye'll stay away from danger. Put on skirts and bonnet, become Patricia for a few days—it won't kill ye, will it? It might save ye. Hide yourself until we've sailed."

That gave me an idea. It was an old trick, but it nearly always worked.

Outside, the icy rain had turned to snow and we left our tracks in it, leading away from our shelter to the boat. Above, the leaden sky was beginning to lighten. Together we dragged the boat out of the tangle of bushes and down to the water's edge.

He held the boat steady as I got in. Then he stepped in and shoved us off, poling with the oars, launching us into deeper water.

The current had us now, taking us out into the dark bay. Not even a fishing boat to be seen. A little wind came up and we stepped the mast and raised the sail, stiff with ice.

"If I were ye," he said, handing me the sheet and taking the tiller, steering us toward Providence, "I would think tonight would be a fine time for a cut and run. But if any trouble is observed from the frigate ye can be sure a gunboat of *Richmond*'s will be launched within minutes to come to its aid. And I won't be able to protect ye."

"So this is it. This is good-bye again."

"A man makes his choice and lives by it, Patricia. Ye dress and act like a man but ye still have a woman's body, a woman's inconstant heart, and a woman's ever-changing mind."

"Inconstant heart? You're the one who shares your bed while I sleep alone."

"Ye're the one who turned me down. The one who walked away in New York. Remember?"

"I didn't turn you down; that's not how it happened. Why must you blame me for circumstances beyond my control?"

"I don't blame ye, I'm just trying to get ye out of my head. To forget ye."

Impulsively I grabbed his wrist as he rowed. "Stop! Don't forget me, Brian, join me. Leave *Richmond* and stay in the colonies. Sail with me, be my partner on *Andromeda*. We can make a good life here, you and I together." We embraced fiercely, the boat luffing up into the wind. It was more of a grapple of wills. For a moment I entertained a hope I had won.

"I'll do what I can to help ye." He reached again for the tiller. Providence now loomed large in the predawn darkness. "But don't ask me to desert my ship. Ye know me better than that, love, do ye not?"

Then it is finished, I thought, my heart as numb as my cold fingers and toes.

Twenty-Six

Providence

Leaving the boat on the other side of the point, beyond the shoal and out of sight of the frigate, we walked up Benefit Street into town, quiet at that hour, the hour before sunrise. The night watchmen had gone home, the tavern drunks had fallen into oblivion, and the ladies of the night had locked their doors and turned out the light. The industrious people—fishermen, housewives, craftsmen, servants—were just waking up to stir the ashes in the hearth, I imagined. The streets were empty but for the occasional foraging pig. The Goddards would be awake I, was certain; a printer's day started early.

"We shouldn't be seen together," I said, but there was no one about. Dalton continued to walk with me along the dark street. When we were a few doors away from the Goddard's, he stopped and gave me the sack of provisions.

"Take this. Ye may need it. A bit of cheese and some biscuit.

Some slops."

I struggled to pull myself together, to regain not only my composure but my very reason for living. To steel myself for what I had to do. Drained of both fear and desire, my spirit felt as damaged as my face. I had no one to blame, certainly not Brian. It was all my doing; I had chosen the wrong course three years ago and the consequences could not be undone. Now I must rally my fighting spirit, my anger, my resolve for the sake of *Andromeda*. The ship was my life, the hope of my future.

"Thank you." I slung the sack over my shoulder, knowing he had risked much for my sake. But I had lost my ship, cargo, crew—and my hard-earned Spanish dollars.

"Take care, Patricia. Stay ashore tonight."

"Adios amigo." I could not possibly say good-bye in my own tongue.

He stepped back into the passageway between two buildings, blending into the darkness. I felt his eyes on me as I walked away, toward the Goddard's kitchen door. Raised my fist and knocked. I turned to look for him, to see his form one last time. I dared not lift my hand to wave.

The door opened abruptly, and Sarah Goddard pulled me inside the hearth-warm kitchen; I breathed in the smells of freshly ground coffee beans and cornbread baking.

"What happened to you, sir? Your face?" She peered at me with a mother's concern; the fine lines in her face seemed to have deepened overnight and her hair was still in disarray beneath her bed cap. At the kitchen table, strewn with ink-stained papers, Mary and Everett were comparing notes, quills in hand, by the light of a half-burned candle. With a great sigh the sleepy-looking servant girl removed an iron skillet of johnnycake from the coals and placed it on a trivet on the sideboard.

"It's nothing, madam. A slight altercation."

"They came here looking for you last evening."

So it was unfolding. I fought a cat's instinct to bolt in blind panic—but where? The gunner had gone back to his ship, to his friends and family. My friends were here in this kitchen.

"Naval officers. And several marines. From the frigate *Richmond*. Wanted to search the house and the shop but they had no warrant and I forbade it; I told them I had no idea of your whereabouts. That as far as I knew, you were a Newport man. I told them you might have gone to Newport."

"The officer I shot has died. They mean to take me and *Andromeda* to Halifax for trial."

All eyes flew to mine.

"Sit down, captain," Mrs. Goddard said, touching my arm, guiding me to a chair. "Let me pour you some coffee. Get you a bite to eat while we determine where we can hide you."

I put down the sack and accepted the coffee cup in both hands, grateful for the comforting heat, the steam rising to warm my bruised face, my ears, numb with cold.

"How did you find this out?" Mary asked.

"I have a friend onboard the frigate. I served as surgeon's mate in her during the war."

"Everett sings your praises," Mary said. "He told us you saved his life."

"Indeed so," said Everett.

"I did what any surgeon would have done." I dismissed the topic, wagging my head. It was my life I must save now.

"*Richmond*'s captain is certain the admiralty court in Halifax will condemn *Andromeda*," I added.

"Is there nothing your friend can do?" Sarah asked.

"He's already put himself in great jeopardy to help me. I can expect nothing further; he'll not defy his captain nor betray his shipmates. *Andromeda* will fetch a good price in Halifax, of which the officers and crew will get a share. The obligations of old friendships only go so far."

"And what of you, Captain MacPherson?" Mary asked. "What becomes of you if they take you to Halifax?"

No one spoke, for all knew I'd likely be hanged.

"We must keep you hidden," Mary said, looking to Everett and then to her mother.

"I can't hide forever, and they'll take my ship to Halifax whether they have me aboard or not. I must take *Andromeda* back, as planned," I said. "I'll take my chances. If I have a few men willing to help me. Tonight."

Everett spoke; he was keen for it. "The stamps are said to be coming ashore shortly after sundown this evening—they'll want to wait until after dark, so as not to be observed. But they'll be met by a mob as they have never before seen. I spent most of the night last night organizing it."

"And what if the stamps aren't brought ashore tonight?" Sarah asked.

"The same men will start a bonfire across the street, outside the courthouse. If they can't burn the stamps, they'll burn a straw tax collector instead."

A knock at the door sent my heart into my throat. Sarah peered out the window then opened the door. It was John Eli, looking just as haggard and unslept as the rest of us.

"I have assembled a small crew," he announced. "They want to be paid for their risk."

"Tonight's the night, John," I said. "*Richmond*'s captain plans to take *Andromeda* to Halifax as soon as possible, I have it on good authority. And I'm wanted for the death of the lieutenant."

John's stubbled face turned ashen. "Then there is no waiting. But how are we to get aboard? Have you thought of that, Patrick?"

"I have an idea," I said. "But it needs fleshing out."

Twenty-Seven

Narragansett Bay

John Eli rowed the four of us in his boat against a light breeze from across the bay. It was a boat he was prepared to sacrifice to the cause. Of the men he recruited, only one had actually showed up at the dock at the appointed time. This young waterman—I didn't know his name and hadn't clearly seen his face—lay in the bottom of the boat, hidden under sail and armed with a musket and a dirk. John had given him a shilling and promised him a crown if we were successful.

John, Everett, and I were dressed in skirts, petticoats, and bonnets belonging to Sarah and Mary Goddard; we had a cask of good Rhode Island rum to sweeten the deal. Under my skirt and petticoat, strapped to my thigh, was a gelding knife borrowed from John Eli, I having lost my pistol to *Richmond*. John also had a knife, and Everett—the better marksman, having served in the militia— was armed with his own pistol. I worried how Everett would manage in a scuffle, with his wooden leg, though he was quite agile on it and, from what I had heard, could hold his own in a tavern brawl. I wondered about my own strength, if pitted against a man's, but knew I had the initial advantage of surprise—not to mention resolve. When something is your own property you fight for it that much harder.

The frigate *Richmond* was still docked at the wharf; she had been seen taking on water and supplies that day, most likely in preparation for departure. Marines on the quarterdeck—I spied two red jackets. Up on the fighting top was another marine, leaning against the mast with a musket at his side. With all the trouble colonists—especially Rhode Islanders—had given His Majesty's ships lately, the captain was maintaining a heightened vigilance. Still, I knew about the sickness aboard that had laid many of his men low. And I knew about the disturbance soon to be staged.

We made no attempt to be quiet and orderly as we drew close to my schooner, anchored out in the bay. Instead, we chattered and jested in falsetto, our breath forming clouds in the chill of the night. We were anxious, each one of us. The smell of our sweat mingled with the scent of the costly French cologne we had doused ourselves with. As we drew nearer *Andromeda*, John plashed the oars and caused the boat to weave, as a man in his cups might do.

"Good evening, gents," I called breathlessly, seeing three figures regarding us from the starboard rail, watching our approach with great interest, muskets in hand. Brian had said there would be four. One man must be below. Sleeping?

"Who goes there?" a young man's voice barked, not at all welcoming.

My mouth went dry and my stomach clenched. "We're ladies of Providence, how do?" I strove for a flirtatious banter, but my voice sounded ridiculous to my own ears, like the neighing of a filly. "I'm called Faith, and these are my sisters, Constance and Prudence." We had decided ahead of time on these rather ironic names. "Such a nice evening, ain't it?"

Silence, but for the click of hammers on muskets. I drew in a sharp breath, my gut twisting in knots. Nothing to do but persist.

"Don't be belligerent. We're just out for a jaunt, looking for some fine randy fellows to share a cask of rum with us. Would you soldiers care for something hot to warm you?"

"We ain't soldiers," one of them said. "We're marines."

Our boat bumped softly against *Andromeda*'s hull. She needed to be scraped of all the barnacles and weed growing at her waterline, I couldn't help but notice with proprietary concern. And a fresh coat of paint; she was beginning to peel.

"Sister Faith, I'm getting a chill," Everett said to me in mock confidentiality. He was in his glory, enjoying this venture, while I was fighting to keep my teeth from chattering. "These fellows don't seem too welcoming. Perhaps we should find our entertainment elsewhere."

We waited, rubbing our hands together for warmth. The guards lowered their muskets but made no move to welcome us aboard or send us away.

"I told you this was a waste of time," John complained in a petulant grumble. "Let's go back to shore and drink the rum ourselves. Or better yet, let's share it with the men on the frigate. That's where the real men are. Hot-blooded men who know what they want and have coin to pay us. The buggers on this flotsam are content with their sorry lot, it seems."

"Yes, let's go back," Everett agreed, and I pretended to vacillate. I could feel the man hidden at my feet shift his weight slightly. The plan was after we three whores went aboard and distracted the men, he would slip aboard to help us with the takedown.

"They have each other for warmth." Everett laughed lewdly.

John picked up the oars again, the oarlocks creaking in the cold air. Above us, the marines were no longer standing at the ready but were leaning against the rail, watching us with curiosity. Now I knew we had them—they were red-blooded men after all.

"Well, adieu, boys. Pardon us for disturbing your peace and sobriety." I touched *Andromeda*'s peeling wooden hull with my hand, pushing us off. "I warned you, girls: They sent the dregs out here to stand watch on the little boat."

Still, nothing happened. We stalled for time, changed positions, pretending to be awkward in maneuvering the boat. If we didn't get aboard soon, it would all be for naught. Once the diversion started on shore the guards would be in a heightened state of readiness. There was no time to falter; there was no second plan.

"Come now, let me row, Prudence. Straight back to the dock to board the frigate; that's where the money's to be made." Everett snatched the oars from John's hands, lowered them into the water and pulled with a weak, uncoordinated stroke

"No, you're no good with an oar," John said in a convincing falsetto. "Move over, I'll row. I told you it was a waste of time coming all the way out here. If only I had something warm to wrap my poor hands around, 'stead of this piece a wood." He took the oars from Everett—they pretended to argue over it—and pulled a few strokes, moving us away from the schooner.

"Sweet, salty dreams," I called out, waving. "Adieu!" The sound of their voices in quiet discussion carried over the water.

Another stroke and we glided farther away. And another. The figures on deck watched us.

"Wait!" one of them called out at last. "Come back, ladies. You'll catch your death of cold. Come on aboard and bring that rum."

Now that the marine in charge had given his permission, the other two red jackets leaned over the rail, calling to us.

"Oh, I can warm you, sugar—show me where you're cold."

"Hey, sweetheart, come on up and let Johnny give you some lovin'. And mind, love, don't drop that rum."

"But do you mariner men have something," I called out, tugging at my bonnet coyly, "to make it worth our while?"

They laughed lewdly.

"Oh yes, my dumplings. Come on aboard, put your hands in my pockets and see what I've got for you."

More sniggers and chortles.

"The rum will cost you extra," I said. "But you best throw us a rope quick, before we change our minds."

"Hold on, my sweethearts, I'll rig a chair. It'll just take a minute. We'll have you warm in no time."

The light wind John had rowed against on the way out had dropped suddenly; a cold fog was forming over the water, which meant for a dangerous escape—if we succeeded in wresting control from the onboard crew.

There was the sound of boom and tackle and then came the canvas sling lowered down from above. I sat on it, gripped the halyard, and prepared to be hoisted aboard. Looking toward shore I could see what I thought might be the bonfire in front of the courthouse. Up over the rail, as the men hauled, and then down until my feet touched the deck. One of the marines grabbed at me but the one in charge pulled me away. "Back off, now, there's two more coming. Let's get them all onboard."

The cask was sent up next, sampled immediately, and deemed fine. Then the chair lowered again. Everett wiggled his petticoated backside onto the canvas sling.

"Heave away, boys," he called in merry falsetto, strangely emboldened by his costume. "Be careful now, you fine fellows, don't let me fall. I'm terrified of heights."

Below us, John made fast the boat and hauled himself up and over *Andromeda*'s rail. "Which one of you three is the biggest man?" he blustered. "That's who I'm lookin' for. You sure there ain't a bigger man for me down below?"

"I'm more man than you can handle," the short, stocky one said. "Don't you worry about going below, I've got what you want."

"Where's the man with the coin? Silver, that's what warms my heart," Everett said, sidling up to the braggart.

"Damn, what's this?" he chortled. "I've got me a woman with a wooden leg!"

"You got something made of wood for me?" Everett answered back, causing them all to laugh.

"I've got something for you, darlin'," the one nearest me crooned, pulling me close. "Come feel this." I snuggled up against him, sizing him up, pressing my hand between his legs to distract him. He was a tall, well-built lad, as tall as I was, and his member was stiff as a plank. Now I pulled my hand away and touched my bonnet coyly, to get my arm in position. There was no backing out now; I let my knee fly with all the power of a mule kick into his swollen groin, swinging my fist into his throat, dropping him to his knees. I grabbed his wrists to pin them behind his back, but he recovered quickly, enraged, and stronger than I reckoned. Snapping his hands down, he escaped my hold on his wrists, spun around and hugged my knees, dropping me to the deck. It was all thrashing arms and legs as we grappled, and he heaved his weight on top of me, pinning me under him. I couldn't move, couldn't seem to draw a breath for the great weight pressing on my lungs. Felt his hands, groping my hips, tugging at my skirts, heard the rip of silk, felt his knees forcing their way between my thighs, spreading them. I fought to free my left arm from beneath the weight of our bodies. My right arm was powerless; he controlled it under one hand, his other hand between my legs, seeking what he wanted, punishing me with his fist.

Like a crazed cat I was filled with mad panic—with wild, blind rage that overcame the pain. I tried to cry out, but there was no breath in my lungs. I thought I would explode with the desire to free myself. All I could move was my head, but it was weapon enough. I brought it up under his chin with all my might, hearing his teeth knock together. Now pulling my right leg free, I threw it over him like a lover, enough to offset his weight. I squeezed him, squeezed my legs together with all my strength, trapping his fist inside me as I pivoted, turned us over, and now I was on top, my left arm free. I drove my fist at his throat but he lowered his chin and my knuckles glanced off. I punched him in the sternum instead, heard him cough, felt him weaken. I leapt off of him, groping in the darkness for my knife.

Around me I could hear the scuffling of bodies as Everett and John struggled to subdue their men. My breath came in wheezing gulps as I slid the blade from its sheath. Fear and rage pumped from my heart and burned through my veins, a powerful combination. My foe struggled to his feet and lunged at me with a roar, knocking me backward, the knife flying from my hand and onto the deck. I fell against the mast, gasping for breath and kicked wildly, as he pressed himself against me, his hands at my throat. Instinctively I dropped lower, grabbed a pin out of the fife-rail at the base of the mast and swung it, hitting the side of his head, feeling the wood impact flesh and bone. He fell into a crumpled heap at my feet.

Ripping my bonnet off my head, I bound his arms behind him with the ribbons and then tied his ankles together with the bitter end of the foresail sheet. I staggered to my feet, looking for John, for Everett. There was a dull pain in my left leg. I grabbed the shrouds to keep from falling. The crack of musket fire, followed by another— had I been shot? I ducked behind the man I had just knocked out. My leg felt strangely numb, but for a spreading warmth I knew to be blood beneath my skirts.

Close at hand, John was in trouble. His pistol had been taken from him and he was struggling to get it back. Where was Everett and his marine?

Our waterman climbed over the rail onto the deck, ducking, raising his musket. No flash, but a shot rang out and I watched him fall. Spying my marine's musket just a body's length away, I dove for it, snatched it close, and rolled back to the rail. More shots. The man from below was now on deck, taking cover behind the cabin. I tried to take aim on John's marine but they were tangled together, so I stepped close and swung the musket, hitting the marine in the back of the head. Now John was free, and armed once again. He pointed to me, indicating I was to sweep the starboard side while he would take the larboard. When I got to our waterman, he was near death, shot in the chest, gurgling in his throat as he drew his last breaths. I squeezed his hand, already cold, and forced myself to move on. I could hear now the shouts and jeers from on shore carrying over the water, a musket fire. Saw John bent over another figure. Everett's marine, alive, gagged with a bonnet and tied to the foremast with the halyard.

We found Everett below, standing over the fourth man, a seaman, bound and gagged.

"Let's get these men into the boat and get out of here." My teeth were chattering, my knees were shaking.

"You're bleeding," Everett said.

Indeed, my skirts were blood-soaked and ripped. I tore off a strip of petticoat and wrapped it around my thigh to stanch the bleeding. Hoping it was only a flesh wound. No time to examine it now.

"I'll be all right. But our waterman is dead."

We lowered the captives into the boat and set them afloat, along with the dead man, wrapped in a sheet of flannel from my own bed. By the time they got themselves untied, we'd be out of sight. Then, slipping our anchor, we set the staysail and the foresail, ghosting away on the current and the barest hint of a breeze. Hearing a pop of musket shots from on shore, I worried for Brian, wondering if he was in the thick of the fracas or if he had remained aboard the frigate. In either case he had compromised his principles and risked his career for me. Our interests, always at odds, had irrevocably diverged. I knew now that we were on opposite shores of a widening river, an unnavigable torrent. Blood had been spilled, men were dead. Would *Richmond* fire on the town?

More gunfire, this time close at hand. The powder flash briefly illuminated a vessel in pursuit of us—almost certainly one of the frigate's boats, being rowed, with a gun mounted in the bow. We needed to make all possible speed now, yet the winds were maddeningly light. Our muskets were useless at this range.

"Head for open water, the middle of the bay," I called out to Everett, at the helm. The current and wind would be stronger away from the shore, and the water deeper. Once the wind picked up and we could set more sails, the schooner would have the advantage over the smaller boat. But a greater speed also meant a greater chance of running aground.

"John, you're at the con. I'll mind the sheets."

It was a challenge even for John, who had grown up sailing these waters, to navigate at night. He looked for the fires on the west bank—fires he had assigned his workers to build at strategic points of land—to serve as waypoints to his plantation dock.

The pursuing boat stayed right on us, neither gaining nor losing ground. I trimmed the sail, trying to squeeze out every bit of speed I could while keeping an eye astern. A yellow flash– they were firing on us. I held my breath but the shot went wide. Another shot, but no hit. And then a voice called out through a speaking horn, commanding us to come to. I could barely make out the words but I knew that voice well. And I knew why we hadn't been hit.

We sailed under the cover of darkness, the bonfire of Providence soon out of sight as we made our way toward Eli's plantation—with John, still in his skirts, bonnet dangling from his neck, at the con, boldly directing to his dock.

The Royal Navy was not easily defeated for long; my old shipmates would be no exception. They had nothing but time on their side. Time—and Parliament. We had not seen the last of them and there would be more frigates and sloops-of-war with more marines and more soldiers to back them up. I knew I was a fugitive from this day forth.

A revolution was in the making, though I couldn't see it then. I had matters more immediate on my mind.

Twenty-Eight

Narragansett Bay

By dawn's light and with the help of John Eli's servants we unloaded the remaining cargo into his barn, covering it with straw. We agreed it would be best if we hid *Andromeda* long enough to scrape her bottom, repaint her hull, and bleach her sails to make her resemble a local fishing vessel.

I spent the following weeks in hiding, up a wooded creek on Eli's plantation, aboard the disguised schooner. The flesh wound in my thigh healed quickly, leaving a pink and rosy scar. The deaths of Cyrus, Lieutenant Markham, and the young man who had been killed helping us take back *Andromeda* gave me much pain. These wounds of the heart wouldn't heal as easily, but there was nothing to do except bide my time until I could make my escape.

My sea chest was gone, along with my clothing and my surgical kit, but the Spanish dollars I had hidden in my mattress had not been discovered. I had money, I had information, and I had connections in Havana.

One afternoon in February, Everett showed up for a visit, bringing me corn muffins, ground coffee beans, and the latest edition of the Providence *Gazette*—still not printed on the official stamped paper, as all of Rhode Island was ignoring the legislation—filled with pertinent news: Virginia had joined Rhode Island and eight other colonies in declaring the Stamp Act unconstitutional. A committee in Wilmington threatened to burn a Royal Navy ship attempting to deliver stamps to North Carolina. Captain Elphinstone had ordered broadsheets offering a reward for information leading to my arrest but neither the Goddard women nor Sam Hall would print them. Still, I was afraid to show my face for I was wanted for the killing of Lieutenant Markham.

"Mary sends this novel by Smollett," Everett said, handing me a parcel. "And Mrs. Goddard sends you this journal, quill, and ink so that you may write your thoughts. Oh, and I almost forgot." From his coat pocket he pulled out a letter addressed to me, care of Mrs. Goddard. It was badly water stained but I saw it had been posted in Newport. Opening it, I found it wasn't from Dominic Hale or his wife or daughter, as I hoped, but from Eos, who reported that the sloop-of-war *Cygnet* was back in Newport—and that they, too, were on the lookout for me. She included a remarkable sketch of Captain Leslie in caricature and entirely unclothed.

I spent the remainder of February in solitude, mending sails and reef points in preparation for the journey, gathering kindling, filling the water barrels with fresh snow, and trying to staying warm by the galley stove. I was fed through the kindness of Mrs. Eli, who sent food from her table. As the month drew to an end I became certain of my condition.

Twenty-Nine

At sea, off the coast of Rhode Island

One morning in March before the sun broke the horizon, I slipped out of the bay with a group of cod schooners, *Andromeda's* deck cluttered with fishing nets and empty barrels. Two Narragansett pacers—gelded yearlings—and eight sheep ready to lamb were housed below in the cabins converted into stalls. The livestock was from John Eli's plantation. Thanks to John I also had three young fishermen, scarcely more than boys, as crew, who all slept in the galley. We stayed with the fishing fleet until we were past Block's Island before breaking off and heading south by southeast, bound for Havana, where the livestock would bring a good price.

One of the lads brought me up a plate of fried cornmeal mush, sprinkled with walnuts and brown sugar and topped with dried apples. It was a dish I normally enjoyed but that morning it made my stomach turn just to smell it. The boy took the tiller while I leaned against the rail and forced myself to eat it. No one knew of the freight I carried. No one knew anything of me at all, except I was their captain and I was to be obeyed.

I missed Cyrus. I missed him for his skill at the helm, for his lively company, for his very presence. I could imagine him now, standing at the helm like he'd been born to it, glancing over at me with his blue eyes sparkling like sun on the water, grinning with confidence, his wheat-colored hair blowing loose in the wind. Cyrus had guessed my true identity, I was certain, yet he had followed my command that night he was killed. He had stood beside me, he had tried to protect the ship and its cargo. He had tried to protect me.

I turned the sandglass to let another thirty minutes run past. It swung on its gimbals with the rhythmic motion of the boat as the grains began to tumble through all over again. Overhead, the sun climbed, reaching its zenith. Time to shoot the angle, calculate and mark our position on the well-worn chart below. The shipboard routines came back, the rise and fall, the ebb and flow. At sea, time is a different thing entirely, marked out by the sandglass, the stars wheeling overhead, the rising and setting of planets and moon.

Standing at the rail, I filled my lungs with the stinging salt air and breathed out, like the tide. Another breath and the feeling of malaise waned, the nausea nearly gone. Belowdecks in the stalls I heard the restless cargo protesting, the impatient stamping and snorting of the horses, the plaintive bleating of the sheep. Deep within my body I felt a flutter, a miniscule earthquake.

Ahead, the horizon was clear, but I knew from experience we'd be reefing down at sunset and that the night would bring its own challenges. Still, with any luck Havana was only a fortnight away—three weeks at the most. I had valuable livestock to sell, and more; I carried the sort of cargo Guyon wanted—goods that took up no room in the hold.

This time, instead of molasses I would buy guns.

Patricia MacPherson
March 21, 1766

Historical Footnotes

Parliament repealed the Stamp Act on March 18 of 1766 but immediately replaced it with the Declaratory Acts in which they asserted total legislative control over the American Colonies.

In 1767 Parliament passed the Townshend Acts, imposing duties on lead, glass, paints, paper, and tea. In 1770, under pressure from the colonies, Parliament repealed the Townshend duties—except for the duty on tea. In 1772 a British patrol boat, the Gaspee, was seized and burned in Rhode Island.

Rhode Island was the first of the thirteen American Colonies to declare independence from Great Britain on May 4, 1776.

Author's Afterword

Women have long gone to sea with men. They were passengers onboard, they worked onboard, they gave birth on board, they died on board. Historically, their presence has been largely ignored.

Patricia MacPherson's character is imagined from my own experiences at sea and as a nurse, as well as from the stories of women of earlier times who found work aboard ship or in the shipping industry.

Hannah Snell was one such woman. Serving in the Royal Marines as James Gray, she was wounded in the line of service, honorably discharged after three years and granted a pension by the Royal Hospital. Snell's story was acquired in 1750 by publisher and entrepreneur Robert Walker, who wrote and serialized her memoir to appeal to a broad English market. For some months Hannah earned money appearing on stage in uniform, singing and performing military exercises. In her life she married three times and bore children.

Another Englishwoman, Mary Lacy, took the name William Chandler, and worked four years as a ship carpenter's servant before apprenticing as a shipwright. In 1770 she took and passed the navy's exam to work as a shipwright. Afflicted with rheumatism, she later applied for and was granted a pension from the admiralty under her given name, Mary Lacy. Mary subsequently married a shipwright and bore children.

The stories of many crossdressing women are harder to verify and have likely been fictionalized or embellished upon. One of these women was Mary Ann Talbot, who began her crossdressing career in 1792 when her guardian, a regimental captain named Essex Bowen, enlisted her as his servant under the name of John Taylor for a voyage to Santo Domingo. She was his "drudge and foot-boy" and presumably his sex-slave—or perhaps a willing mistress. When Bowen tired of having her as his foot-boy he proposed enrolling her in the regiment as a drummer. When Mary Ann objected, he threatened to have her "conveyed up the country and sold as a slave." (From *The Life and Surprising Adventures of Mary Ann Talbot, in the Name of John Talyor, A Natural daughter of the Late Earl Talbot as related by Herself.*)

Many more stories and ballads of crossdressing maids aboard ship or serving in armies were written or sung, and I believe there is at least some truth to most of them. These women had their own reasons for choosing the lifestyle, and while we can speculate it was for economic reasons, for adventure, for patriotism, or to be with a loved one, we'll never know for certain.

There were also women, many more women, aboard ship who weren't pretending to be male. Girlfriends, wives and prostitutes were allowed aboard navy ships when the vessel was in port but ordered off when the ships were ready to make sail. A few occasionally stayed behind, belowdecks, and out of sight of the officers. Here they shared their protector's biscuit and hammock in exchange for giving him warmth and comfort on his off-watch hours. These invisibles occasionally are mentioned in the ship surgeon's records or in a sailor's memoirs.

Wives of warrant officers often accompanied their husbands to sea. They were given special permission to be onboard; the ship was their permanent home. These women helped keep an eye on the young boys serving as servants, apprentices, and midshipmen. They served the gun crews as powder runners and assisted the ship surgeon and his mate during battle.

Several historical figures make an appearance in this novel and in the previous Patricia MacPherson novels. In *Rhode Island Rendezvous* the young Alexander Hamilton appears in Christiansted, St. Croix, living with his older brother and his mother, Rachel Faucette Lavien, as he did in real life.

But it's Rachel's story that interests me. Ron Chernow brought much of it together in his biography of her youngest son, *Alexander*

Hamilton. Chernow raises some doubt about the identity of Alexander's biologic father—an ambiguity I've allowed to surface in my novel. More importantly to me is the strength and resilience of the woman who raised and provided for Alexander and his older brother nearly single-handedly, as her protector James Hamilton was absent for extended periods and without means.

Rachel deserves to have her own story told in full—as does Mary Katherine Goddard, American publisher, bookseller, Baltimore postmaster -- and the first to print the Declaration of Independence with the signers' names typeset in the *Goddard Broadside*. While I have imagined and invented the roles Rachel and Mary Katherine play in my novels and their relationship to the fictional Patricia MacPherson, I have tried to be true to their accomplishments and the spirit of their lives.

About the Author

Linda Collison's composite career includes critical care and emergency nursing, teaching skydiving, volunteer firefighting, and writing. With her husband, Bob Russell, she has sailed thousands of nautical miles, many of them aboard their sailboat *Topaz*. The three weeks they spent as voyage crewmembers aboard HM Bark *Endeavour*, a replica of Captain James Cook's ship, sparked her interest in maritime history and inspired the acclaimed Young Adult novel *Star-Crossed* (Alfred A Knopf; 2006) which evolved into *Barbados Bound; Book 1 of the Patricia MacPherson's Nautical Adventure Series*, adult historical fiction.

For more information about Collison's writing and her forthcoming books: visit www.lindacollison.com
Twitter: @lindacollison
Instagram: lscollison
Facebook: BecomingPatricia

Photo Credit: Sheila Zappanti

Barbados Bound—Book 1

Portsmouth, England, 1760. Patricia Kelley, the illegitimate daughter of a wealthy Barbadian sugarcane planter, falls from her imagined place in the world when her absent father unexpectedly dies, leaving her no means of support. Raised in a Wiltshire boarding school far from the plantation where she was born, the sixteen-year-old orphan stows away on a ship bound for Barbados in a brash attempt to claim an unlikely inheritance. Aboard the merchantman *Canopus*, under contract with the British Navy to deliver gunpowder to the West Indian forts, young Patricia finds herself pulled between two worlds—and two identities—as she charts her own course for survival in the war-torn eighteenth century.

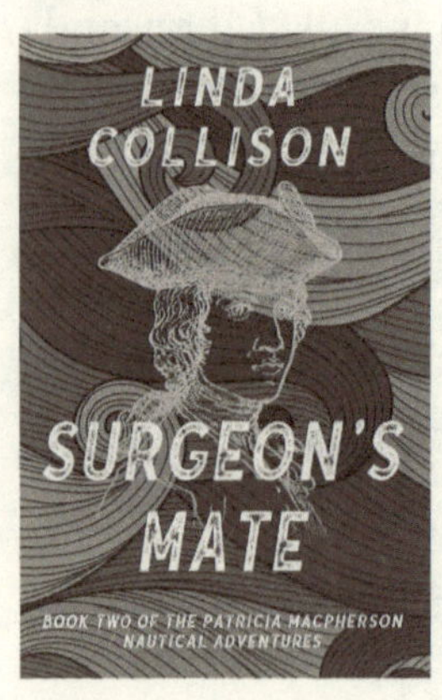

Surgeon's Mate—Book 2

Patrick MacPherson is a surgeon's mate—but he's not the man he claims to be. Born *Patricia*, the illegitimate daughter of a wealthy Barbadian sugarcane planter, the privileged girl falls from her imagined place in the world when her absent father unexpectedly dies, leaving nothing but debts. Raised in a Wiltshire boarding school, with no other family or connections, the gangly sixteen-year-old brashly slips aboard a merchant ship bound for Barbados, embarking on a desperate journey to find her place in the world. The journey is one of unexpected transformations; Patricia becomes Patrick—ship surgeon's mate—but how long will the ruse last?